continued . . .

"Here is a sequel that many MaryJanice Davidson fans have anticipated . . . The Wyndham werewolves ignited a spark in many hearts, and the result is this phenomenal story."

—*Romance Reviews Today*

Undead and Uneasy

"Breezy dialogue, kick-ass action, and endearing characters."
—*Booklist*

"Be prepared to fall in love with the Undead all over again! I can't wait for the next book!"   —*Romance Reviews Today*

Undead and Unpopular

"Think *Sex and the City*—only . . . filled with demons and vampires."   —*Publishers Weekly*

"This is simply fun, no two ways about it."   —*The Eternal Night*

Undead and Unreturnable

"Cheerily eerie 'vamp lit' . . . A bawdy, laugh-out-loud treat!"
—*BookPage*

"No one does humorous romantic fantasy better than the incomparable MaryJanice Davidson."   —*The Best Reviews*

Undead and Unappreciated

"The best vampire chick lit of the year . . . Davidson's prose zings from wisecrack to wisecrack."   —*Detroit Free Press*

continued . . .

Undead and Unemployed

Undead and Unwed

Anthologies

CRAVINGS
(with Laurell K. Hamilton, Rebecca York, Eileen Wilks)

BITE
(with Laurell K. Hamilton, Charlaine Harris, Angela Knight, Vickie Taylor)

KICK ASS
(with Maggie Shayne, Angela Knight, Jacey Ford)

MEN AT WORK
(with Janelle Denison, Nina Bangs)

DEAD AND LOVING IT

SURF'S UP
(with Janelle Denison, Nina Bangs)

MYSTERIA
(with P. C. Cast, Gena Showalter, Susan Grant)

OVER THE MOON
(with Angela Knight, Virginia Kantra, Sunny)

DEMON'S DELIGHT
(with Emma Holly, Vickie Taylor, Catherine Spangler)

DEAD OVER HEELS

MYSTERIA LANE
(with P. C. Cast, Gena Showalter, Susan Grant)

MYSTERIA NIGHTS
(includes Mysteria *and* Mysteria Lane, *with P. C. Cast,
Susan Grant, Gena Showalter)*

Wolf at the Door

MaryJanice Davidson

BERKLEY SENSATION, NEW YORK

THE BERKLEY PUBLISHING GROUP
Published by the Penguin Group
Penguin Group (USA) Inc.
375 Hudson Street, New York, New York 10014, USA
Penguin Group (Canada), 90 Eglinton Avenue East, Suite 700, Toronto, Ontario M4P 2Y3, Canada
(a division of Pearson Penguin Canada Inc.)
Penguin Books Ltd., 80 Strand, London WC2R 0RL, England
Penguin Group Ireland, 25 St. Stephen's Green, Dublin 2, Ireland (a division of Penguin Books Ltd.)
Penguin Group (Australia), 250 Camberwell Road, Camberwell, Victoria 3124, Australia
(a division of Pearson Australia Group Pty. Ltd.)
Penguin Books India Pvt. Ltd., 11 Community Centre, Panchsheel Park, New Delhi—110 017, India
Penguin Group (NZ), 67 Apollo Drive, Rosedale, Auckland 0632, New Zealand
(a division of Pearson New Zealand Ltd.)
Penguin Books (South Africa) (Pty.) Ltd., 24 Sturdee Avenue, Rosebank, Johannesburg 2196,
South Africa

Penguin Books Ltd., Registered Offices: 80 Strand, London WC2R 0RL, England

This is a work of fiction. Names, characters, places, and incidents either are the product of the author's imagination or are used fictitiously, and any resemblance to actual persons, living or dead, business establishments, events, or locales is entirely coincidental. The publisher does not have any control over and does not assume any responsibility for author or third-party websites or their content.

PRINTING HISTORY
Berkley Sensation trade paperback edition / October 2011

Library of Congress Cataloging-in-Publication Data

Davidson, MaryJanice.
  Wolf at the door / MaryJanice Davidson.—Berkley Sensation trade paperback ed.
    p.   cm.
  ISBN 978-0-425-24311-4
  1. Werewolves—Fiction. 2. Vampires—Fiction. 3. St. Paul (Minn.)—Fiction. I. Title.
PS3604.A949W65 2011
813'.6—dc23
                                                                        2011026406

PRINTED IN THE UNITED STATES OF AMERICA

10   9   8   7   6   5   4   3   2   1

For the readers who have been asking
for this since Derik's Bane.
All right, enough already!
Seriously: thank you. Without you I might not ever
have gotten a chance to write this,
and what a dreadful thing for the Wyndhams,
trapped inside my head!
No one should have to live in my head.

~• ACKNOWLEDGMENTS •~

Thanks as always to the hardest-working people I know: my agent, Ethan Ellenberg; my editor, Cindy Hwang; and my assistant, Tracy Fritze. I deserve none of them. And yet, they're trapped with me, endlessly, endlessly trapped. They must have done something dreadful in past lives. Lucky for me!

Also to my family, who never get bored with boring other people about the awesomeness that is me.

My husband, for cheerfully tolerating the awesomeness that is me.

My children, for resisting their genetic proclivities.

My readers who, incomprehensibly, keep reading.

Thanks, y'all!

—MaryJanice Davidson

I keep the wolf from the door

But he calls me up

Calls me on the phone

Tells me all the ways that he's going to mess me up.
—*A WOLF AT THE DOOR*, RADIOHEAD

I've got my dead stepmother working for the devil, I've got the *devil*, I've got my sister (the Antichrist), a half brother who's teething like a moray eel, I turn completely evil in the future, my friend won't stay dead, and my husband has been withholding sex since he found out I kill him once the magic's gone. I don't have time for werewolves. Besides, they're fine. They're hanging on the Cape, they're doing werewolf stuff.

—BETSY, QUEEN OF THE VAMPIRES

Everybody has a secret world inside of them. All of the people of the world, I mean everybody.
—*THE SANDMAN*, NEIL GAIMAN

~•~ AUTHOR'S NOTE ~•~

This book takes place after the events of *Undead and Undermined*. Probably. Betsy's pretty sure. "Look, shit's going down, all right? What am I, a walking, talking table of contents? I've gotta raise the dead and maybe shoot my sister between her baby blues. Stuff's *happening*, okay?"

For Michael Wyndham's backstory, see *Secrets*, vol. 6, "Love's Prisoner," and *Secrets*, vol. 8, "Jared's Wolf."

For Derik's backstory, see *Derik's Bane*.

For Boo Miller and Eddie Batley's backstories, see "The Incredible Misadventures of Boo and the Boy Blunder," from *Kick Ass*.

Also, the yuck-o jobs Eddie mulls over came from "Ten of the World's Worst Jobs," www.oddee.com/item_96873 .aspx. Talk about small blessings.

Prologue

The werewolves were holding hands. They did not share kinship by blood or bond; their relationship was more like a protective secretary looking out for her clueless boss. Her extremely clueless boss.

The female leaned over and spoke softly in his ear. She wasn't trying to be secretive. The werewolves across the table could hear every word. "We've been through this before."

His nostrils flared. "*You* have."

"And I'm still here."

He seemed to take courage from that, from her neat designer suit, her unmarked face, her unchewed ears and dark eyes. "You're still here. And so am I." He glared across the table and she caught an unpleasant whiff . . . a cactus catching fire, maybe. Strong and sharp, enough to make the eyes water.

"Remember the rules," she reminded him. Her hand was beneath the table, so the other werewolves couldn't see her nails digging into him.

He swallowed a gasp and nodded. The rules. Right. Show no fear. Ideally, *feel* no fear. If you do, don't show it. If you absolutely can't help showing it, make the fear about something else. Anything else.

"Ow, my suit!" he yelped, and showily yanked her hand away from his lap. "My wife'll kill me."

"Nah," one of the wolves across the table said. "She won't."

"Be worth it, though," his partner said, leering at her blunt, small hand and unpolished fingernails. Rachael resisted the urge to make an obscene gesture or put one of his eyes out with her thumb.

"Won't be anything left to kill, anyways," his partner added, and they wee-hawed together like two of the three little pigs. Wee, wee, weeeee-haw!

"Quit that. *Anyways* is wrong, just like *towards* is wrong." Oh, boy, she hated *towards*. More than plague, she hated *towards*. "Don't get me started. Now if you two are through chortling," Rachael snapped, "maybe we could get some work done?"

The werewolves, a little taken aback by the feisty tone, had a quick huddle at their end of the table ("She's so little!" "Chortling? Who says *chortling*?"). Then they manned up ("Shouldn't it be wolfmanned up?" "Why are you asking me these things? What's wrong with you?") and slammed down several thick folders bristling with Post-it flags. The least jarring color was a queasy pale green.

The burning cactus smell intensified, and her client slapped his hand on the table, hard; the *crack!* got everyone's attention. "You need to understand . . . this is vital. You understand me, boys? I'm talking life or death here. Critical shit." Their ears pricked forward. "Our records are one hundred . . . percent . . . accurate."

"Balls."

"What he said. This audit's been coming a long time," the older werewolf said, jabbing his thumbs at (weirdly) himself. "You've had years to get your shit together, years of half-assing it, but now time's up. Now you gotta fight or flight." He smiled. "And everyone in the room knows you're not so good at the fight part."

As one of the people in the room who knew that, Rachael said nothing. Her client spoke instead. "I'm ready. We're prepped; we can go anytime."

"Oh-umm?" The younger werewolf paused, and Rachael smiled at the sight of him sifting scents and trying to match them to the wrong sounds. "You are? I mean, you can?"

"Sure." It was amazing, she thought, how someone could smell so utterly different from one second to the next. The smallest boost to his confidence, and burnt cactus changed to orange bubblegum! "I just thought . . . I mean, I thought Michael . . ."

At the name of the Pack's leader, all four werewolves eyeballed each other while pretending they weren't. Rachael Velvela was in the room because she was Michael Wyndham's cousin.

That was bad news for Tom Fritzi of Fritzi's Fried Funnel Cakes (FunCakes™), who had been audited with a vengeance yet at first had no idea who she was. He'd hired her because he thought her last name was Velveeta and was so fond of fake cheese he kept her on after he realized the mistake.

The toads across the table, lesser beta-males, had audited Fritzi for the chance to get close to a relative of the Pack leader, and also because they hated FunCakes™. (They were neutral on the issue of processed-cheese food.)

So here they all were.

"I can't stand suspense, and maybe you can't, either, so I'll just come out with it. My cousin isn't popping in for a cameo." Rachael was already bored with the proceedings. She had been hip deep in Fritzi's finances for the last month and could actually smell FunCakes™ coming off the files. "He's busy running the (were)world. And since there's no point in waiting for him, we might as well get started."

So the blood-soaked nightmare that was the audit of Fritzi's Fried Funnel Cakes, Inc. (seventeen locations nationwide) began.

One

❧❧❧

"There's no easy way to say this. There's not even a cool, clever way to say this. So I'll just come out with it. I need you to move to St. Paul indefinitely and keep an eye on the vampire queen."

Rachael had suspected nothing when the summons came. In fact, she had assumed the Pack leader, Michael Wyndham, was wishing her a belated happy thirtieth. He was notorious for remembering significant dates about seventy-two hours too late. It was possible to time him. Sometimes he would round up all the cousins for a big b-day blowout that left the little ones in sugar comas and the adults reaching for sunglasses long before the sun rose high. Could a werewolf get a hangover? Sure. How much booze did it take? Gallons.

But he'd had his hands full with the newly discovered

vampire issue (vampires! In Minnesota! Thousands! Controlled by a moron who loved designer shoes!), so she thought nothing of never hearing from him three days after her birthday. She loved her cousin, but he had many responsibilities. As, of course, did she. Tax season was nearly upon them.

So she had suspected nothing when she drove to Wyndham Manor (how too, too aristocratic East Coast!), once a monastery, now the seat of North American werewolf power and home to several generations of Pack leaders.

The monks must have had a keen eye for architecture, mood, and luxury, for the pile of deep red bricks they had abandoned (or had been turned out of and devoured . . . history was not Rachael's gift) was truly castlelike.

It was built of enormous red bricks and stones, with a dazzling number of windows on all sides, sweeping porches, turrets, multileveled decks, swimming pools (idiotic, given that the Atlantic was right behind the mansion), miles of private beach, and even a golf course. Not that she played; it seemed too much like fetch.

She herself liked to drive out here in her blue Kia Rio when her Change was upon her. She liked to park in the private lot on the beach below the bluffs, Change, then race up the cliff until she was looking at the back of the mansion, nearly always abandoned because her Pack had all Changed and gone away.

Then she would trot around to the immense green lawn in front of the manor, a lawn so wide and deep it was like a dark green lake, one that would take her a while to swim across. She'd flop on her back, wriggle to work out some kinks (human form to wolf form left a nagging ache in her vertebrae), and look up at the bright, bright stars while the wind groaned in her ears and everywhere there was the smell of the ocean, so salty and strong and alive it was almost like the smell of fresh blood.

Now here she was, being packed off like an embarrassing relative ("Away to the sanitarium with you, crazed Aunt Petunia!"), and who knew when she'd be able to roll around on that green lawn, that lake of grass. The stars in Minnesota couldn't be as big, or as bright, or as clear. No oceans. The Land of Ten Thousand Lakes had no oceans.

Lakes often smelled like dead fish.

And *he* wouldn't be there. Michael, her Pack leader and, always more important, her cousin and friend. Her protector. Sending her away when he had many stronger and rougher and smarter—all right, maybe not smarter—but there were literally hundreds of werewolves who would *leap* at the chance to scout and sneak and spy. But Michael wanted her to go . . . and for what?

She opened her mouth and coughed; for the moment, her throat had been too dry to speak. She tried again. "Spy on the vampire queen?"

Michael winced a bit at *spy*, and from his furtive manner, he was clearly hoping his mate, Jeannie, couldn't overhear any of this. It was also probably why the door was closed. Jeannie Wyndham hated intrigue or, as she sometimes called it, *werewolf sneakiness*. Also, from what Rachael had seen and heard,

Jeannie *liked* the vampire queen. That was . . . difficult to swallow. Not that there was anything, uh, wrong with the big blond woman from Minnesota . . .

"Keep an eye on," he said again. "Okay? Keep an eye on. That's all. I've already arranged for you to rent a house in her neighborhood—"

"Rent?" She tried, but not very hard, to keep the sharp tone out of her voice. She hated renting. Land was the only thing they could not make more of; owning property was the way to go. It had been true a thousand years ago, it had been true five hundred years ago; it was simply that the masses teeming over the planet knew that, now.

Her *cousin* knew that, now.

"Rachael, I'm sorry." He spread his hands and gave her a wry smile, no teeth. Werewolves were terrible at deceiving each other, and she and her cousin had grown up together. She knew he was sorry.

She didn't care. Because she knew what he was sorry for, and it left her unmoved.

I'm sorry I'm sending you away from your home and everything you've known. I'm sorry you have to leave your lands. I'm sorry I'm making you uproot your life for my whim du jour. Sorry, sorry, so sorry, hey, you want to go play with my kids while I explain that to keep their way of life safe I have to uproot yours? No? Maybe another time.

Or maybe never.

"Rachael, your house here on the Cape will always be yours.

It passed to you when your mother died; it will be yours, and your children's, and theirs (assuming that part of the Cape doesn't drop into the bay) forever."

Well. That was something, at least. She restrained herself from sniffing.

"While you're away we'll take care of maintenance, send someone out to shovel and mow, get in there for some light cleaning every month or so, pay your utilities, keep the lights and phone going . . . things like that."

"That's the least of it," she replied, and he nodded. It was. He was a billionaire. He could keep a thousand houses going with electricity and garbage service. It wouldn't take up much of his time. It wouldn't take up much of his assistant's assistant's time. "What if I can't get established in Minnesota? All my clients are from around here, and I'm only licensed on the East Coast. Super-sneaky paranormal intrigue is one thing, but I have to earn a living. I have to be able to fund," she finished, "my super-sneaky paranormal intrigue. Which isn't covered by my CPA."

Her licensing issue was a result of her mother's insistence, years ago, before she died. Probably died. They'd never found the body, and if Rachael learned one thing from reading comic books, *they gotta find the body*.

Gah, she could actually hear the woman. Had for years . . . before she (probably) died. "Why limit yourself to Massachusetts? What, because most of the weres in this country are here? What, you'll never need to help the family in, say, New Hampshire?"

Sound advice, but it hadn't covered the Midwestern states, so right now, she couldn't, either.

"We'll get you licensed for Minnesota. Paperwork's already in motion."

"No doubt," she said dryly.

He shrugged and kept his expression neutral. They were close kin, but he *was* still her Pack leader. Just because he had never, ever asked her to jump before did not mean he never would . . . or that she never would.

She studied him while he droned about licensing and software and boys who mow. It was funny how, the older he got, the lighter and denser he got. When they were kids, his hair was jet black, long, and curly. He started getting gold streaks in his teens, streaks that exactly matched his startling yellow eyes.

Now in his thirties, his hair was the dark gold of an autumn sunset; he remained one of the few men on the planet who could pull off a mullet. (Perhaps the only . . . ? But that could be mere Pack loyalty.)

The older he got, the less like one of *them* he looked. Funny how the humans never noticed. But then, as a species, they weren't known for such things.

Lucky for us.

". . . and your laptop goes everywhere. What's the difference between a living room ten blocks from here and a living room in a rented house in St. Paul?"

Oh, let's see. Ambience, lighting, wallpaper, smell, windows, carpeting . . .

"Same laptop, same software, right? You've been telling me for years you hardly have to visit your clients face-to-face anymore."

And now to pay the price for candor.

"You already get everything electronically, right?"

"Mmmm." This was Rachael's way of saying, *Dammit, I know there's a flaw in your stupid plan, and when I figure it out, I'm giving you a ground-glass suppository though I will obey you anyway because that's how we do things around here.*

"And you won't be on twenty-four/seven."

"On the vampire queen?" Ugh.

He nodded, jerking a gold wave out of his eyes. "If you need to fly back here to meet a client or see one of us or, I dunno, pick apples or something—"

"Pick *apples*?" When in the blue hell would she ever turn to tourist agriculture? *If I kill him, I have to kill Lara, too, and then Jeannie will shoot me in the face, which will ruin everyone's weekend.*

"—someone will keep watch on the queen while you're gone."

The flaw! Not only was she being sent away, there would occasionally be a blundering werewolf she didn't know and probably didn't want to know stumbling through her rental house, making messes, and generally being a pain in her sometimes-fuzzy hindquarters. When she returned to St. Paul, it would doubtless be to clean up whatever mess he or she left.

Wherever you are, Mother, you're laughing, aren't you? Even as an infant, Rachael had disliked having her things moved around. Back then, her only weapons had been poop, pee, and drool, and she had heartlessly wielded them. Mighty had been her poops of wrath.

"The economy's still pretty bad," she added with more than a little warning. "You might not have noticed, O Mightily Wealthy Pack Leader, who never once worried about a meal in his spoiled silly life—"

He started to grin, then his gold brows rushed together and he did a credible job of looking stern. Too bad he didn't *smell* stern. He could fool the *sapiens*, he could even fool werewolves who didn't know him very well. He couldn't fool family, ever.

She was trying to stay annoyed, but the truth was, she loved Michael Wyndham and would do what he asked, no matter how annoying or time-consuming or stupid or dangerous or irritating or inconvenient.

Her earliest memory was of falling through the ice of a cranberry bog not even two miles from where they were having this annoying conversation. It would have been her last memory, but her tall cousin leaned down with his yellow eyes blazing and, with a mittened hand that held hers so hard he broke two of her fingers, yanked her from the awful cold water and the dreadful freezing sucking mud.

She scowled, hoping to cover her out-of-character sentimental journey. She would do as he asked but had no interest in making the asking part easier for him.

He saw her look and again held up placating hands. "Aw, Rache, give me a break. Can't help it that the Wyndhams have never missed a meal. It's my fault they went into lumber at the exact right time in the exact right part of the country? You remember Aunt Forcia?"

Rachael made a determined effort not to giggle. *Must . . . remain . . . unmoved . . . Must exude . . . hatred . . .*

Aunt Forcia had loved sheep. Loooooved them. During full moons, she'd pull down as many as she could and just gorge. Then she'd pass out on the side lawn for a week or so. The cousins had all thought it was hilarious. (The sheep, less so, but it was a werewolf-gobble-sheep world. At least it was in Cape Cod.)

"You know perfectly well you'll inherit a chunk of our ill-gotten gains in another generation or so. You'd have it now, even!" At her eye roll, he continued. "Your mom asked me to keep most of it in a trust for you until—"

She knew the parameters of the will and waved that away. Being wealthy was complex and annoying, caused too many questions, and created too much paperwork. She supported herself very well as a CPA. Let the money remain in trust for another decade; she truly did not care. Perhaps if she had cubs someday she would change her mind, but it wasn't likely: changing her mind, or having cubs.

"Look, even if you weren't a blood relative, we wouldn't let your house crumble into ruin, no matter where you were in the world doing your duty for the family, and no matter how long it took."

"My duty for the family." She said it in a flat tone. She, like her cousin standing before her, was a werewolf: *lupi viri* (strictly translated to "men of wolves" . . . When was Latin going to get with the program with their female tenses?).

And the *lupi viri* gave their habits not much more thought than the *sapiens* pondered their humanity. When *sapiens* pondered anything. And weren't dreaming up more excuses for global devastation. A less potty-trained species she had never met in her life. There was a perfectly good reason most werewolves stayed in Massachusetts, and it had nothing to do with all the beaches. Or the Freedom Trail. Or the New England Aquarium.

"So that's what this is, Michael? My duty?"

"It's not just that I need someone to go out there. I need someone who wouldn't go solely out of duty. Rache, you're one of the smartest people I've ever met. You're blood, too. But you're a better choice because . . ."

"Because . . ." His scent, which had been a mild and unwarlike vanilla, suddenly shifted, and now she could smell dry sea grass, a lot of it, ablaze.

Ah. Here came the precautionary tale.

"Rache, I can't lie to you." It was true. He was a dreadful, laughable liar. "The last person I sent out there died in the vampire queen's service."

Two

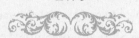

Rachael had known that, had been expecting that, so it wasn't the shock Michael had feared.

She remembered the incident well, and the memorial afterward, on the occasion where they'd had the chance to meet the queen and her consort. Rachael hadn't gotten more than a glimpse, or much chance to hear the trial—Wyndham Manor had been crawling with thousands of her kind—but regardless of what little she saw, she still found Betsy Taylor silly beyond belief.

No one had especially liked the late Antonia Wolfton (except Derik, Michael's best friend), but they'd all been angry that a werewolf had died on a vampire's watch. And what the hell kind of a name for a monarch was Betsy?

"I need someone smart, someone I can trust, who can take care of herself—they don't have any cranberry bogs out there for you to fall in—"

"Ha, ha, O Rotund Pack Leader."

"Back off, I've only gained a couple pounds since Lara started all that ruckus. Do you know how many boys have been following her home? She's in goddamned elementary school and the boys are already trotting after her! I'm gonna have to start beating them off with sticks!"

"The terrible trials of our magnificently round Pack leader."

"That's all sheathed in sculpted muscle, Rache." He patted his (to be fair, reasonably flat) stomach. In fact, Rachael was pleased to see evidence that he was able to relax enough to indulge now and then. Before his mating, before his cubs came, he had the lean look of a man always too close to a bad mistake. Jeannie and the children had changed all that.

It occurred to her, again, that he had changed in other ways. Usually when she saw him, there were dozens of others around, usually the cousins and their kin. She couldn't remember the last time she had been alone with him. So things she normally never thought of were not only occurring to her, she was thinking of them again and again. Things that had changed . . . and things that never changed.

His looks, for instance. In addition to the change in his coloring, there had been changes to his very nature . . . external and out. He'd been narrow and lean until adulthood, all gawky elbows and long legs. Maturity had helped him grow into a powerful body. He might have relaxed enough to dodge workouts, but he could still put his fist through the trunk of a tree, could still squeeze a rock into gravel.

His eyes, though . . .

His eyes had always been a savage gold, rare and striking even among their kind. From the moment he pulled her from the bog, she knew this boy would be the greatest Pack leader in the history of the *lupi viri*. And no matter what had happened to the Pack since then, no matter the deaths and births and matings and Challenges, his eyes had *never* changed.

No, Michael Wyndham was in the right place, the right Pack, and she knew it, and nearly everyone else did, too.

Oh, sure, there were scuffles now and again, mostly in the early years. Jeannie Wyndham, mother of Lara, the future Pack leader, was involved with at least one. *That* had been humbling for all of them. A *human* coming to Michael's rescue and saving them all with time left over to bitch about how chilly the manor got in the darker corners . . . ah, the shame of it . . .

Now, years later, as an adult male in his prime (to be fair, the males tended to be bigger and stronger with no effort on their part, though she disliked distinctions by gender), his no-longer-black, no-longer-long, now-shoulder-length dark gold hair had a ripple of a wave through it, and when he stepped into sunshine, it often looked to her as though he was blessed by the sun god; their Pack leader was dazzling, which was annoying.

He had no idea. At all. No idea that to her, to the Pack, he really did seem as something of a living god. And that was annoying, too. She could hear herself thinking such nonsense and wanted to roll her eyes. Unfortunately, knowing it was a cliché (and a silly one, too) did not make it untrue.

He snarled at her, showing a lot of teeth, but it was more show than substance, he was still trying to articulate what he needed from her. Her! One of his least fiery, passionate, ferocious Pack members. One who never married, one who kept to herself, had never left the state of Massachusetts except for one ill-fated trip to New York City. One who didn't seek people out.

Come to think of it, she would go because Michael knew all her flaws, knew she disliked fights and intrigues, knew she was more *sapiens* than any other Pack member, knew she was happy at spreadsheets. She would go because Michael *knew* all those things about her . . . and loved and valued her not despite her odd habits, but because of them.

Her father and Michael's father had been brothers born a generation apart. Her father loved to read, loved to figure things out, loved to learn, loved to teach.

Michael's father loved to fight.

So here they were, two branches of the same tree, but for all they had in common, there were many differences, too.

"Listen: I don't think they mean trouble for us. Specifically, I don't think Queen Betsy does. I don't know what her consort wants . . . that fucker's harder to read than my own dad was."

Yow. Not a lightly made comparison. Her uncle had been famous for sitting quietly one moment with a cub in his lap, then exploding into a fight to the death after tossing said cub to a bystander.

Her irritation at the rude uprooting of her business and personal life—

What personal life, you silly bitch?

That's enough out of you, inner voice who sounds like Mother.

—began to fade, and interest began to take its place. The interest wasn't necessary, but it was a bonus she was grateful for. Because the two people in this room knew she would leave at once for Minnesota, despite the dreadful seven-month winters.

Of course she would go; there had never been a doubt. If it meant her death, fine. If it meant permanent banishment from her homeland followed by death, as it had for Antonia, fine. If it meant tedious meetings and bad food and shrill vampires and dreadful weather and frostbite and a thousand tornadoes (they had all sorts of them in Minnesota, right?) and having to eat lutefisk and lefse so as to blend in, and to march through the monument to consumerism that was (drum roll, please, or maybe a cow bell?) THE MALL OF AMERICA . . . so be it.

But she was a family member first, a werewolf second, and an accountant third. Aw, nuts. If her mom was still alive, she would have given Rachael a smack. Mother had always thought her only daughter's priorities should be different.

But! Mother was (probably) dead. So Rachael's priorities were her own.

And it suited her fine.

She would go. He was family; more, she loved him like a brother and was bound, not only by their blood, but by her heart, to do as he asked.

But it would never do for Michael to know too much of that, so she fumed and scowled and insulted him and let herself be placated and pretended this thing was a terrible inconvenience.

Oh, wait. It *was*.

Dammit!

Three

"Everybody has a secret world inside of them. All of the people of the world, I mean everybody. No matter how dull and boring they are on the outside, inside them they've all got unimaginable, magnificent, wonderful, stupid, amazing worlds. Not just one world. Hundreds of them. Thousands maybe."

Eddie Batley groaned and tossed *The Sandman* across the surgically neat living room. Then he gasped in horror at his foolish, foolish act and hurried across the spotless blue carpet and retrieved the graphic novel. Ennui was no excuse, *ever*, to abuse anything by Neil Gaiman. Ever.

He blew on the cover but it was relievedly flawless.

Ever!

His (un)dead roommate, who would have heard a carpeted

version of *The Sandman* hit carpet in the deep (carpeted) vacuum of space, yelled from the back bedroom, "Rule six, Eddie!"

"Ed*ward*," he muttered back.

"Rule six, Ed*ward*!"

Vampire hearing. Argh.

(Rule six: no hurling graphic novels before five thirty P.M.)

"I need to get out of here."

"Where would you go?"

"I'm talking to myself out here, if you don't mind."

"Rule eleven!"

(Rule eleven: before five thirty P.M., talk to yourself in your head.)

"Rule twenty!"

(Rule twenty: back off Ed*ward* if you've brought up two or more rules before supper.)

Edward waited, but Greg ("Gregory, dammit!") Schorr was finished.

It wasn't Greg(ory), anyway. It was him. It was Edward Batley IV, heir to a long and distinguished line of accountants. He had to get out of there. Being a third wheel for a few months was almost fun. Fodder for late-night routines (which Greg loved, being the only vampire comedian on the planet, probably), right? Something to blog about, yes? He should have pitched the idea to Hollywood; all things paranormal were being turned into terrible movies and terrific sitcoms. He could move out to California, pitch screenplays. There were worse ways to make a living. Guard at Buckingham Palace. Brazilian mosquito researcher. Portable toilet cleaner. Roadkill remover.

That would all have been fine, except for the tiny detail that it hadn't been months. He had been a third wheel going on four years. No, that wasn't . . .

He whipped out his cell, stabbed the calendar button, and gaped with horror at the date. It hadn't been going on four years. It had been four years and seventeen days. Boo would never allow a party, never mind a simple, "Hey, thanks again for saving me from being devoured and turned into a shambling Night Thing," but he always made a mental note of the day they'd met.

Four years and seventeen *days*? That was nothing to blog about. It wasn't almost fun anymore; it wasn't something to pitch to public access, never mind FX. It wasn't an undead *Three's Company*. It wasn't even *Wings*, or *Coach*. It was more like an *I Love Lucy*, if Lucy was a vampire slayer and Ricky was a vampire, and Fred had divorced Ethel because of her vain, snoopy competitiveness but lived with Lucy and Ricky anyway. In Boston. And was an accountant for Grate and Tate.

I have to stop seeing my life as a series of old sitcoms. And *I have to get out of here.*

And go where?

That was it. His enemy wasn't just ennui; it was the sweet, sweet comfort of knowing where the strawberry Smucker's was, and when Boo and Gregory were out at a comedy club so he could enjoy, um, alone time, and when they were getting drunk enough so he could hear their slayer/vampire sexual shenanigans from half a block away. (The first time he'd realized what he was hearing, he simultaneously popped a boner and threw up. Boo was hot; Gregory was hot if you were into sculpted urbane intelligent vampires; and they were both terrifying.)

He liked most everything else about his roommates; they were always a good time on a Friday night, and sometimes they let him come hunting with them. He liked knowing he was paying next to nothing for his share of a gorgeous Quincy apartment (Jack had moved in with Chrissy and Janet for a reason, right?), and where the best black-and-white cookies were, and when the Tuesday staff meetings were safe to skip (which was every third Tuesday). And yeah, like he'd said, he liked his roommates, too. It would be weird, being in the Boston area and not living with them.

Also, they'd miss him dreadfully.

"Pathetic," he announced.

"Seriously, will you stop? Rule eleven!"

He ignored Greg(ory) and pointlessly began tidying the spotless apartment. Boo had always been one to let a bra fall where it may, but he and Greg were sticklers. Edward suspected it was his mind, which tended to stray toward all things tidy (you could perform an appendectomy in his cubicle). And Greg was old-fashioned. *Really* old-fashioned. "Cleanliness is next to you-know-what," he'd informed them the first week he had moved in. When Boo had realized he was serious, she laughed like a hyena for ten minutes. Then they'd disappeared into her bedroom for . . . uh . . . never mind.

He swiped nonexistent dust off the coffee table in front of the squat black-and-white TV, circa 1950 (Gregory liked his antiques, and Boo didn't give a shit), and thought about his living situation. Despite the lack of a plasma TV and windows *not* curtained in dark brown, it was pretty sweet. He couldn't believe he was considering leaving. Well. Considering considering leaving.

Who are you kidding?

Good question. He stayed for the reason he stuck with anything in his life: he needed a kick in the ass to get going. So far, kicks in the ass were in short supply. Worse: if not for the third-wheel thing, it would likely never occur to him to move out. His roommates were the most feared vampire slayer (not that Boo would ever, ever refer to herself as such) in the history of time, and a dead comedian who lived (so to speak) for the slayer.

What could compare? Honestly? A corner office at Grate and Tate? The newest toy from Steve Jobs, the iAll? Regular sex with Uma Thurman (provided he could overlook the man-hands and man-feet)? To quote a sage of the age, "Shyeah!"

Also, they had a view of Wollaston Beach. A tiny sliver of a view they could only enjoy during high noon with clear skies on Thursdays, but still. Water view! In Boston!

So he stayed.

"I'll live here until I die," he announced.

"Which, if you don't stop breaking rule eleven, will be later this evening."

Edward did not have a heart attack, or jump back, or even flinch. Although he never heard Gregory coming, years of cohabiting with a dead guy had given him a flinch-free poker face.

"Nothing's going to make me move out," he announced.

Gregory yawned and headed for the kitchen.

"Not one thing."

"So, who asked you to leave? We found this place together, you, me, and Boo," Gregory said mildly. "No reason not to make use of it as long as you like. Half of it is yours, after all." He opened the fridge, withdrew several oranges, plugged in the juicer, and began shredding orange after orange. Edward had never seen anyone fonder of fruit juice. Maybe it was a vampire thing.

"My place is here."

"All right."

Edward yawned, showing too many teeth that were too big. He was a tall, lean man with a tendency to slouch, Columbo style. His dark blond hair was pulled back in a ponytail, though he occasionally clipped it savagely short. Or cop short, which made sense, as he'd been a member of the BPD in the years leading to his death.

"You realize you get this way every several months."

"Do not."

"You need a woman, my friend."

"Tell me about it." Problem number thirteen: the only women he met were off-limit coworkers and psychotic vampires. On the occasion he met a perfectly nice, good-looking, intelligent woman, his lifestyle freaked them out. Frankly, if it didn't freak them out, it would have freaked him out. And to be fair, he hadn't been trying terribly hard to hook up. Chalk it up to more of his ennui. Or sheer laziness.

"Where's Boo Bear?"

"Dare you." Gregory stopped chugging his orange juice long enough to point at him. "I *dare* you to call her that to her face."

"It would sure solve a lot of problems," he said glumly. He slipped into one of the bar stools at the kitchen counter and propped his chin up on his elbows. "What, is she out on recon?"

"Stop that. I loathe pop culture gibberish. And yes, she is researching Amanda Darryn for me."

"The Black Widow." Like the villain played by Joan Cusack in *Addams Family Values*. Except this one had been getting married, vacuuming bank accounts, and killing her husbands for a hundred fifty years.

"Soon to be The Staked Widow." Gregory had disliked being murdered and returning from the dead. He coped by honing his routines and tracking down really, really bad vampires. As a former cop, his contacts and data access were inspiring. He had hired Boo to slay a local vampire who specialized in murdering third graders. Boo had been pissed, then intrigued, then horny. Cue the happily ever after theme. "Would you like to come? Perhaps you merely need to get out of the house."

"So there's another vampire to kill next week. A flood of the undead."

Gregory snorted. "That's the spirit. And I stand by what I said: you need a woman."

"You say that about everything wrong in my life."

"Because it would fix everything wrong in my life." He busily squeezed more oranges—Edward wondered why he bothered with a juicer at all. The man could flatten grapefruits with either hand. Except Gregory was beyond fastidious. Case in point . . . "Aaaah!" He grabbed a sponge from the sink and scrubbed off the wayward seed, hurriedly dumping it in the sink. "Have you ever seen anything more repellant?"

"You're asking someone who's never missed a Comic-Con."

"I do not know what that is. Ah! Here comes the sun of my life."

Edward, of course, couldn't hear anything. But he wasn't surprised when, a minute later, he heard Boo's key in the lock and the thud of the door popping open as she kicked the bottom. Edward had never seen her turn a knob in his life.

"Darling!"

"Moron." She was shrugging out of her leather jacket in mid-bitch, tossing it over the back of a kitchen chair and walking right up to Gregory for a kiss. It was a long one. Edward looked away, thinking, *You'd think they hadn't seen each other for a month.*

"Hmmm, let me guess." She leaned out of his embrace and licked her lips. "Orange juice!"

"You must be a detective or something."

"Or something," she agreed. She plopped into the bar stool beside Edward, squinted at him, then said, "Are you still doing the can't-go-but-don't-want-to-stay-but-shouldn't-go thing?"

"It's not a *thing*," he said, offended. "It's midlife crisis."

"You're twenty-three."

"Boys mature faster than girls," Gregory said, pouring a glass for Boo. "That's a medical fact."

Boo laughed and shook her hair out of her eyes. A striking woman, she had the coloring of a true albino, so pale she seemed almost to glow. Her skin was so light it appeared fragile, as if it would tear like paper. Her hair was also white, and curled under at the ends, the curls bouncing around her shoulders. Her eyes were such a pale blue she appeared blind, or jaded, as if she had seen much to blast all the color from her face and body and soul.

He called her Boo, but her street name was Ghost. She'd gotten into the slaying because not one but two vampires had tried to kill her before her twenty-first birthday. Her striking coloring was like catnip to them. Long ago, she had decided to make herself bait, the better to stake you with, my dear.

He still remembered how she'd explained because of her skin, she had to stay out of the light, too. She was treated as a freak. She preferred evenings, and her senses were heightened from long years of avoiding sunlight. There was nothing supernatural about it, or her, but try telling anyone else that. It had taken Edward almost a year to believe that about her.

"I've never seen an ugly vampire," he said out of nowhere. Boo and Gregory both looked at him. "Isn't that weird?"

"No," they said in unison. Gregory waited, but they didn't illuminate until he coaxed them with a "What?"

"All vampires are essentially murder victims."

"Most," Gregory corrected, mashing more oranges.

"Fine," she replied. "And given a choice of murder victims, they go for the cute ones."

"That's like saying a rapist picks victims based on their sex appeal," Edward protested. "It's not about sex. And with vampires it's not about looks, it's about blood."

"And beggars can't be choosers," Boo agreed. "But when they can, they go for the pretty ones. No offense, Greg."

"I *am* fairly fabulous," he admitted with a modest smirk.

"So: murder victims." Boo slurped more juice, then grimaced and pushed the glass away. It made a small damp ring on the counter; Gregory gasped and wiped it up in the manner of someone getting rid of nuclear waste: get it out, get it out, get it out, *out*, OUT! "Agh, too much acid on an empty stomach."

He prompted her: "They go for the pretty ones . . . still sounds dumb."

"They die, they come back. Some return more vengeful than others, which is why I have a job. Some of them spend decades making innocent people pay for what a killer took. Then I have to kill them. So, essentially: it's all about me, in the end."

Edward was astounded. He had never heard her speak like this; usually Boo's attitude was the only good vampire was a dead one, except for the one she was shacked up with.

"None of which explains your whole should-I-stay-or-should-I-go thing. You want to go? Great, sounds like a plan, drive safely and don't forget to update your Facebook page."

"I'm touched," he said dryly. "But I'd never do that to either one of you. You're not up to the emotional devastation that'll be caused by my moving out." She snorted, but he affected not to hear it. "Besides, what would you do without me? Your lives would be as drab and lifeless as a *Jersey Shore* rerun."

"That's not quite—" Gregory began.

"The Team Supreme with its own laugh track shall go on!" he declared. "I would never leave either of you."

"And here we go with the threats," Boo observed.

"Nothing would induce me to leave this teeming coastal area infested with the undead and leave you defenseless. Nothing!"

Then he looked at the mail.

Four

"Well." Rachael squinted as she took in the situation. "No matter how many times I look, it's always the same. Minnesota is . . . just . . . awful. I don't know why anybody comes here unless they've lost a bet."

"I'm sorry to hear that," the head of the St. Paul Chamber of Commerce said politely. "Permit me to suggest it might grow on you."

"Like a fungus, Mrs. Cain?" *East Coast snob*, she chided herself. *Yet, Minnesota sucks*, she reminded herself. "Wait: I know a Cain from the Cape. I do her parents' taxes, if that's them." Given how teeny the werewolf community was on the planet, never mind the 413 square miles of Cape Cod, she fully expected the answer to be yes. She'd made a bad first impression and felt guilty enough to engage in polite small talk, but not quite guilty enough to apologize for being an ass. Yet. "Are you related?"

"It's a family name; she's my cousin."

"Cane as in candy?" *My God, I'm bored already.* "Cain as in . . ." *What friggin' difference does it make?*

"Cain as in the first murderer."

"Uh." Rachael's theology was a little rusty. "What?"

"From the Bible. You know: 'What hast thou done? The voice of thy brother's blood crieth unto me from the ground.'"

"Ohhhh. *That* Cain. Thanks for clearing it up."

"Not a problem . . . may I ask what specific aspect of the Land of Ten Thousand Lakes disagrees with you?"

"The fact that there are eleven thousand eight hundred forty-two lakes, to begin with. Every license plate is wrong. And it's freezing, no one can tolerate these temperatures and live."

"It's sixty-eight degrees."

"It's August!"

Rachael shifted her weight from foot to foot. It was rude to stand there, almost looming over the wide red oak desk and its occupant, a heavy-set woman with skin so deeply black her red earrings played up her mahogany highlights and queenly cheekbones. In fact, the woman was so zaftig and beautifully dressed, Rachael wondered what she was doing there: the woman could have made big bucks in front of any camera.

The president of the chamber or, as Rachael thought of her, *el Diablo*, cleared her throat, which drew attention to the crisp cream-colored blouse and deep V neckline of the moss green suit.

"We're having a cold snap."

One that's lasted ten thousand years, she thought but did not say. She took the newsletter out of the purse sack and smoothed it out with her palms. "Listen, I'm aware it's a stereotype to come to the Northern Hemisphere and complain about the weather. I'm sorry I made an appointment to come shit all over your home state. I really am." She wasn't, but it wasn't the other woman's fault. Rachael resented having to be there at all; *there* could have been Honolulu. "I just wanted to let you know I was in town on Pack business—"

"Yes, about that—"

"—and have no idea when I'll be leaving, except I'll keep you updated. And I'm guessing that since you knew I was coming, you've already set up a place for me to live. Thanks in advance."

"I think you'll really like Summit Avenue. Did you know it was voted one of Ten Great Streets by the American Planning Association? And there are mansions that were built back in the early days of the city? Several of the homes were built between 1890 and 1920."

"I did not know that."

"See?" She looked triumphant. "That's just *one* of the fascinating bits of history to be found in St. Paul. There's all sorts of things you'll be better able to explore on your own, things like the governor's mansion being right there and the fact that three of the homes are on National Historic Landmarks."

Wow. "I will, uh, try to get right on that." The woman sounded *just* like a Frommer's. She'd either been working there too long and ended up sounding like a poster on a travel agent's wall, or had always talked like that and therefore was born to run a chamber of commerce, any chamber of commerce. "That all sounds swell. So, I'll head over there next, get settled in . . . What is it, an apartment?" Cain nodded. "And I'd better figure out a good time to meet their . . ." Rachael rolled her eyes. "Vampire queen, gah, it sounds way too Comic-Con to me." Though just knowing when to reference geeks at Comic-Con probably meant she spent too much time at Comic-Con.

"We use Pack as a personal noun, and our Pack leader (can you hear the capital letter?) lives in a mansion anyone can just drive right up to. And we occasionally allow fights to the death to determine the status of the males, which they normally don't do on Election Day around here."

"Glass house. Got it." She was even in one, sort of . . . the chamber of commerce building was sizeable and chock-full of windows. She could see why the woman chose to work in the modern building, full of sharp angles and shiny metals. One entire side was almost all windows, a big half-moon of windows.

"Have you ever met her?" Rachael asked. She took out the newsletter, which showed the creases from being read many, many times, from her purse bag. This one was a deep cream, with the Burberry logo and font in black lettering. "Even in passing?"

"I have not. There was never a strong enough reason." Meaning as an envoy from the Pack leader, or seeking vengeance for a blood debt, or being a welcome wagon rep, everyday things like that. "I suppose I didn't need one so much as I was (and still am) a little vague on the protocol, so . . ." She shrugged.

"She puts her address and phone number on a newsletter with a circulation of six figures, and you were worried about protocol."

Mrs. Cain mulled that over, then laughed. "Well, yes, if you put it that way . . ."

"So, I'll go see her." She folded up the newsletter and caught a flash from one of the stories: "Top Ten Reasons Why You Shouldn't Pull Some Lame Vampire Crap from the Movies." Interesting topic. Not for the first time, Rachael wondered if the newsletter was a satire. "Like I said, I just wanted to drop by."

Mrs. Cain nodded at Rachael's bag. "Did you lose your purse?"

"Never had it." She cinched the bag shut. It was the sturdy, protective bag designer purses came in. She took a perverse pleasure in collecting and using the bags, but not the handbags themselves. She supposed there was something wrong with her.

"We very much appreciate your courtesy." Mrs. Cain spoke for herself and the dozen or so men and women who worked for her. Packs within packs; happened all the time. Humans did it, too, they just weren't as aware of it.

"Don't mention it. Courtesy is my meat and drink. And even as I'm saying that, I'm realizing how full of crap I am."

"Don't let me keep you."

"Don't worry."

Five

"This!" Edward shook the newsletter in front of his bemused roommates. "*The Overbite*, the monthly vamp-goings-on newsletter, which, for some reason . . . let's just say I can't imagine what we did to get on the mailing list."

"That's a good question," Boo said. "Maybe you have to know someone, and we do, even if we don't know we know them. And did either of you notice when I began sounding like Dr. Seuss?"

"Exactly! Who do we know? And are they dangerous?"

"Seriously, Eddie. Greg. It's really starting to bother me."

He ignored her. "It's all text, a bunch of little articles . . . see? 'Top Ten Reasons Why You Shouldn't Pull Some Lame Vampire Crap from the Movies.' And I think this one's an ad:

'The Antichrist is looking for soup kitchen volunteers.' Soup kitchen volunteers! It's gotta be a code for, I dunno, the end of the world or something. It *does* means something, though. I know it. And here!" He flipped the page over and tabbed a finger at the article on top. " 'First Aid for the Undead,' by Dr. Marc Spangler. And this: 'I See Dead People: Keep Your Cool When the Dead Won't Leave You Alone.' The only thing in here that isn't weird is the photo of the high heel." He squinted. "I guess somebody named Fendi took this picture and wanted it in there."

"All this to say . . . ?" Gregory prompted.

"If it's fake, it shows the workings of a dangerously cunning mind, one that should be investigated in order to protect society. If it's true, there are *vampires* in St. Paul, actual blood-sucking, Vlad the Impaler, allergic-to-cross-and-garlic, unholy creature, dread-denizen-of-the-undead *vampires*!" He reread a section on the back page. "And they're having a potluck on the third."

"I'm a dread denizen of the night," Gregory admitted.

Boo laughed and tackled him; they both flopped onto the striped sofa. "I've never held that against you."

"That is a lie! You've always held it against me, you've just repressed it."

Boo wriggled around until she was half on and half off Gregory. Edward turned to put the pitcher of juice in the fridge, and when he turned back, Boo was lying almost full length on the couch, her head thrown back, and Gregory had started whispering in her ear and nibbling on her throat. Not literally, thank God. Okay, yes, literally, but not hard. Carefully, even gently. It was really skeevey to watch.

And lonely.

But also skeevey, dammit!

"Who better to go check it out? Nobody ever sees me coming; if it's false, then no harm done. I'm only out a little time. If it's not, I'm already best friends with a bona fide who-ya-gonna-call vampire slayer. It works on multilevels, big number one being that I need a change of scenery, and you two can stalk and stake jerkoffs almost as well without me."

Gregory snorted against Boo's neck, which made her laugh out loud. At least, he *thought* it was the snort. "Almost, yep, right on all counts, good work! We'll try to stagger along without you."

"Because we're so brave," Gregory added in mid-nibble. "We'll gladly put everything at stake for you."

Boo, who had begun kissing him, stopped at once. "You'd better pretend you didn't make such a shitty pun on purpose," Boo warned.

"Oh, I do. I do."

"My work here is done," Edward announced, waving the newsletter. Boo said something. It might have been, "Mufff unnggh." Or, "You still here?"

"I mean it. I'm out of here. Gone, zip, out the door and

onto the bitter brutal streets of a St. Paul suburb. You're not going to have me to kick around anymore," he threatened.

They seemed fine with it. Which sort of summed up his problem: there was no place for him in this apartment, town, life. Okay, *life* was a little strong, but now that he'd begun actively exploring his ennui, he was shocked at how much there was, and how it'd come to be there so long.

It wasn't like he woke up and increased his carbs in order to fatten up so he could migrate. It had been a long time coming and, in a way, had nothing to do with Boo and Gregory. Was it on his roommates that he'd been hypnotized by routine?

No. Just like it wasn't on them that finally, after four years, he was awake.

"Awake . . . and vowing to bring the light of justice to flush out the dark corners of the undead!"

"Could you pick up some milk while you're at it? Skim if they've got it, otherwise two percent."

I've got to get out of here.

It wasn't exactly *Let's be careful out there* or *Avengers assemble!* but he'd take what he could get.

Six

Five days later . . .

It was fate that led her to the Woodbury Barnes and Noble that night. Fate, and an urgent need for both a lemon scone and *Newsweek*. Later, Rachael was unable to remember when exactly she'd spotted Edward in the store, because she hadn't started to pay attention until the felony assault. But she always remembered the first thing he had said to her, right there in front of the *Sweet Valley Vampires* display: "The undead really, really dislike being this popular."

That was odd enough to catch her attention . . . and he was cute enough to keep it.

Like any werewolf, she had started sorting scents the moment she came through the door, categorizing and filing them away. She did it as automatically as people checked the rearview mirror when they backed up. And when she focused on Edward, it was the way people didn't pay attention to the color of a necktie until they were right in front of it.

So it was with Edward's scent, a pleasing combo of clean cotton and oranges, with a sprinkling of underarm deodorant; she liked it right away. She also liked the way his light brown hair was a bit shaggy, in need of a trim, and she liked the way the ends of his hair kept trying to curl under. Best of all, she liked his shirt: "Your Favorite Band Sucks."

"I suppose they would."

He was staring at her. She wasn't sure why; he wasn't a werewolf. She knew this as people know who was into the Cheetos because of their orange fingertips.

She repeated herself, louder: "I suppose they would."

"Who would?"

What was he staring at? "Would what?"

"Who would . . . Wait. What?"

"Let's start over." Actually, she should just walk away . . . Why draw out this encounter? But she didn't want to, and she didn't know why.

Then she did know. He was an attractive, intelligent male and he was in his sexual prime. The beast in her thought the chances with him weren't just outstanding, they were almost a necessity. She was a creature of instinct and senses, as different from this man as the great apes he'd evolved from were different from the wolves in her old, old family tree. *I suppose that means while my instinct is to bring down prey, his is to make tools!*

Her civilized side thought it might be fun to go get a Frappuccino with this guy. Her beast wanted to lure him to her lair and have sex all afternoon.

"I'm so sorry, I honestly wasn't paying attention . . . I have no idea what I actually said. I was kind of in my own head." He paused, then added with the air of someone sharing a great, shameful-yet-exciting secret, "I'm in there a lot, actually."

"I know exactly what you mean." She extended her hand and almost gasped when he seized it and wrung it, as if he was afraid she'd change her mind about introducing herself. "I'm Rachael Velvela."

"Vell-vay-luh? That's neat." Neat? He thought it was neat? No one had ever said that. People just immediately started mocking it. She'd been Rachael Velveeta from kindergarten on up. "Edward Batley. It's really nice to meet you." His pleasure and attraction were apparent, and increased hers. "I come here a lot, but I don't remember seeing you before."

"I just moved here from Massachusetts." She never said Cape Cod. She was startled by how many people had no idea where that was. Most of them knew where Massachusetts was. "I thought I'd come in and pick up a few local guidebooks to sort of look around."

She would never tell this cute, great-smelling stranger the

shameful truth: she thought Summit Avenue was one of the most beautiful streets she had ever seen. The mansions were breathtaking and each one was more beautiful than the last.

She had thought the rows of mansions were lovely the day it rained. Then the sun came out, the late summer light slanting down and illuminating the gorgeous detail of those great, great homes from the past. *Mrs. Cain, how right you were.*

"So I was in the travel section, and then this man told me the undead don't like all the attention they're getting."

"Yeah, uh, sorry. Can't believe that was out loud. Of course it's all bull—it's not true. I mean, it *might* be true, it *would* be true, if there were vampires in real life. Which there aren't. At all. Because if there were—and there aren't—I'd never be so careless as to wander around random bookstores telling strangers the likes and dislikes of the blood-drinking dependant."

"The what?"

"Or the breathing-impaired . . . whichever you think is, you know, not offensive."

"I can't tell if this is the silliest conversation I've had all week, or the most interesting."

"You want to get a blueberry scone, maybe sit down with an iced tea or something, try and decide?"

She smiled at him. "Well . . . yeah. I would, actually. Except that the taste of blueberries makes me vomit, so I will take a lemon scone."

"Usually when I talk to a girl," he confided, "she doesn't use the word *vomit* until we're trying to pick out which movie we want to see."

She laughed so hard she nearly walked into the endcap. Guidebooks to St. Paul, handsome strangers using odd pickup lines, and baked goods produced by the Starbucks Corporation . . . could there be a sillier, funnier day?

Seven

Could there be a scarier, worse day?

Edward thought not. He had been surveilling the mansion occupied by the queen of the vampires for the last two days, two days of *lies*. Two days of lies, betrayal, and cruel funhouse mirrors. The more normal and Ansel Adams–esque the picture was, the worse it was to realize it was more like Charles Addams.

He had been staying at the AmericInn Hotel in St. Paul Park, a cute little city just a twenty-minute drive from Summit Avenue. And every day he went out to get a look at the enemy's burrow. He was proceeding on the assumption that the newsletter was real, that it was all real.

Of course you are, you always do . . .

That's true, but this time it was a safety issue, he told his inner voice. Given the subject matter, he figured it was much safer to err on the side of caution. If it all turned out to be a lie, some silly or mean lie to stir things up and make mischief, at worst he was out only a few hours of his time and what little money the disguises cost.

And it was bound to be a lie. And that was a terrible thing. Not because he thought the human race was in trouble from some secret vampire uprising (although that was always a theoretical concern, he figured that when it came to the undead gaining mastery over the earth, a zombie apocalypse was much more likely).

No, he didn't fear that . . . at least, not much. But as for what he *did* fear . . .

Boys and girls, gather around and I'll tell you a story.

The thing was this: all that stuff? That weird paranormal *Twilight*-ey shiny weird vampire stuff? *It was all true.* But that wasn't even the huge thing.

The huge thing was, *it wasn't all that exciting.* The huge thing was, *people accepted vampires and vampire hunters as neighbors.* The huge thing was, *people in your building didn't care if you were dead as long as you didn't stick Canadian nickels in the dryers.*

And if the weird cool shiny stuff was true about vampires, didn't that call into question the "mythology" of things like fairies and werewolves and leprechauns and mermaids? That meant there was a whole *world* out there, not just one he'd never been able to find, but one he didn't know existed. It proved that although he felt his life had been full of undead shenanigans with Boo and Greg, it was just a sliver. Just a tiny bit. And the thought of how big it all really was, the dreadful sensation that it wasn't the shark fin but the shark . . . *that* was terrifying. *Iceberg right ahead!* terrifying. And he was fresh out of James Camerons.

Boo said nay. Boo and Gregory said assuming vampires proved the existence of werewolves was like assuming plumbers proved the existence of accountants. And they should know, since Greg had been, in the course of his seventy-two years, an accountant and a plumber. (Also a bookstore clerk, a ship's captain, and a travel writer.) He'd seen things, terrible awful things. Polio and U.S. Customs and early-release copies of V.C. Andrews books (talk about the fierce undead!). Greg saw those things, knew those things; he ought to know about this.

But maybe it wasn't true. And if it wasn't true . . .

Right! So he was off! Or, in this case, back to the scene of the crime(s).

He had worn khaki pants, a red shirt, and a tool belt the first day. He knew he could pass, at a glance, as a utility worker and a Target employee. In this way he was able to skulk in the back lawns, the lawn of the undead as well as the ones on either side of it.

And what a yard! A gigantic yard, a wonderful yard. Nobody had yards in Boston; they had oversized postage stamp–shaped parcels of land with grass and hostas growing on them. And this yard had a fence, wrapping around the whole thing like the ribbon on a Christmas present. No cool sinister iron doors swinging shut with the shriek of rusty hinges *(Eeeeennnnnhh-hhhh!)*, but the old-fashioned black bars were good enough.

There was a garden shed and lilac bushes and, on the left, a croquet set. He didn't want to think about the terrible things the vampire queen could get up to with a croquet mallet.

The second day, he wore black jeans, a black long-sleeved dress shirt, and his old black sport coat. Black tennis shoes and black socks . . . it didn't go, but he was hoping no one would care enough about him to get a look at his footgear. Who cared about what kind of shoes you wore to a neighborhood skulking?

He'd dressed up a little because, if he was stopped today, he'd play Lost Business Guy. Summit was only a few blocks away from all sorts of offices, plus there was a Catholic school and a junior high on the street itself.

Besides, he felt more comfortable in dark clothing, even in late afternoon (he had been sleeping in each morning and staking out the Summit Avenue Crypt in the late afternoon and early . . . very early . . . evening). He was sure no one had put his aimless wandering together with a supposed Target employee who had been called to recommend what kind of lawn chairs went with a gigantic mansion built in the eighteen hundreds. But that didn't mean no one would ever spot him, or have questions for him. Thus, the black clothing. It was almost impossible to work up a really good lurk in pastels. It went against nature.

Today he had seen a few more people come and go; it was busier than last night. The big fat black girl, and a dark-haired guy wearing scrubs. Oh—whoops. Not fat; pregnant. Maybe her obstetrician? Anyone who lived in a big old gorgeous mansion like that could afford her own fleet of doctors, so it only made sense to—

Oh my God.

Was the vampire queen growing her own army of evil babies? The undead couldn't have children, could never know the thrill of suckling life from within, that noble calling, that utter demand from our species that we replenish and replace our population. Could the nefarious woman decide in her own ghastly way that, cheated of ever suckling life, she in turn would cheat other women? Perhaps . . . a score of women? Perhaps . . . perhaps he normally couldn't use *suckling* twice in thirty seconds, and was that a good thing or a bad thing? Probably an irrelevant thing.

He peeked through the branches of a lilac tree and watched the pretty, dark-skinned expectant mother and her (imprisoned? blackmailed?) obstetrician-to-the-damned and gasped with the horror of it. Even in his worst imaginings, he never thought there would be an army of enslaved evil babies to contend with.

Maybe it'll only be one enslaved evil baby. Maybe that baby's special . . . or the mom-to-be is.

That was when it had stopped being more fun than worry. In fact, that was *exactly* when it became more worry than fun . . . he was scared.

And stupid. Until he saw *her*, he hadn't truly appreciated the cost to the innocents. It had been more game than mission: try to find out if the newsletter is real or just a big tease; try to get an idea how many numbers the mansion had; try to find out what these Minnesotan vampires were up to.

Now, though. Now he just wanted to tattle on the vampire queen to Boo and then step aside while his best friend got her feet wet.

Eight

Which brought him to the Woodbury Barnes and Noble. Of all the days to meet somebody potentially cool and *thoroughly* hot. Yeah, this day. Of all the days to think maybe picking up and moving to a patch of the corn belt wasn't insane. Yeah, this day.

Now here she was, all kinds of cute . . . and from the Cape, too!

It might be no coincidence. Perhaps fate has pushed us together, into this modern-day watering hole. Perhaps fate is working through a retail coffee chain to get the kind of scone that doesn't *make this girl throw up.*

"Do you believe in fate?" he asked her.

The hotness that was Rachael Velvela sipped her Green Tea Frappuccino. "Next you'll be asking me my sign."

He could feel his face get warm as he flushed. "Yeah, not too lame and dated, right?"

"It could be worse," she teased. "You could have asked me if I needed sexual healing."

Ohhhhh, I wish she hadn't said that. Just what I need: a five thirty P.M. *boner.*

He was surprised it hadn't happened earlier. Rachael had the most beautiful freckles he had ever seen. Her hair was a rich dark brown. *A color to make a sable tear out its own fur in jealousy!* Okay, so dark brown. Her skin was lightly tanned, enough so it looked like she went out and about in the summertime but didn't obsessively lay out on beaches and frequent tanning salons. She had over a dozen freckles sprayed across her nose and cheeks, the kind that increased in summer and sort of hibernated the rest of the time, and lovely dark eyes that tilted just a little bit at the tips. Her eyes almost exactly matched her hair.

She made her tank top and cardigan and jeans look like wedding finery. He had lived for several years with a woman who never bothered with makeup, and could see Rachael didn't, either. So it boggled the mind to wonder how gorgeous she could be if she sat down and *tried.*

But! He would not be distracted. Because a simple let's-get-acquainted question had become much more important to him. "I'm serious: do you believe in fate?"

"The jury's not in yet," she said after a long moment. He had the impression she was giving the question serious thought, really taking her time to come up with the right answer, or what would be the right answer for her. "A week ago I had no idea, none, that I'd move my entire life to Minnesota."

"Get out. Wow, *no* idea?"

She shook her head.

"Well, jeez, I hope nobody got hurt or sick in your family . . . It's none of my business why, but—"

"No, no, that's all right." Another Splenda-infused sip. "I'm sort of in the family business. And when my cousin says go, we go . . . the whole family's dependant on us going to work when we're supposed to, and on doing a good job. So it might be inconvenient and arbitrary, but it's also important. After all," she added, smiling, "I get access to the company checking account. It wouldn't be fair if I expected all the perks and none of the work."

He had bought a slice of pound cake and a chocolate and banana smoothie (she had insisted, nicely but firmly, on buying her own snack) but was too excited to touch either one. "So you just picked up and relocated? Just like that?"

"Exactly. Relocated. Yes."

"Have you ever been away from your family before?"

"Not for more than a few nights. Most of us—well, there are two kinds of families that live on the Cape. The ones who have kids who can't wait to leave and never come back, and the ones who have kids who never leave. Guess which ones we are?" She laughed and shook her head. "It's only now that I'm out here that I realize what a scared little country mouse I've been. Complaining and wanting to scurry back to my hole." Rachael's upper lip actually curled, like she was a fox about to bite. It was cute *and* scary, an interesting combo. "Pathetic. My cousin wouldn't have believed it to see me. But I didn't expect . . . everything's really different."

"Do you miss them?"

"Oh . . . miss them?" She blinked her big dark eyes at him, like a sexy Bambi. With weirdly sharp canines—she obviously wasn't a vamp, but she sure had a cute overbite. "I haven't really been gone long enough to . . . well . . . I guess if I think about it . . . yes. I miss them."

Her smile widened . . . and then she burst into the fiercest tears he'd ever seen.

Nine

"You did *what*?"

"Don't talk like I've gone insane. I had to dump the body."

"Ah . . . insane? Don't be silly. Body dumping sounds very sane to me."

"You've got that *tone* again. What, you think I'm gonna be dim enough to drive around with a dead body in my trunk?"

"But surely—the other one—"

"Yeah, well, I gotta step it up, okay? Nobody noticed the other one. At this point, I don't care *who* goes up in flames, you got me? It can be any one of you . . . doesn't matter who. It'll still solve all my problems."

"All of them, eh?" She would believe *that* when she saw it. "We agreed this needs to go away."

"We sure did. And this is how it's gonna happen. Quit acting like I enjoy this shit; you know I don't. So are you gonna help, or are you gonna create more problems for us?"

There was a long silence on the other end of the phone, followed by what might have been a sigh . . . of frustration or sorrow or fury, he didn't know. She wasn't close enough for him to see it.

He supposed he had some sympathy for her. A little. On the other hand, she was hardly lily-white on this whole thing. He firmly believed there was no such thing as a victim.

He also believed no one was innocent. Not past the age of five, anyway.

Another sigh, followed by, "All right. Yes."

Then she helped him, as he knew she would. Poor dumb bitch . . . didn't she know the first thing the bad guys always did was get rid of the assassin?

Not his problem.

Whistling, he headed back to his rental car, twirling the key ring around on his index finger and wondering how soon he'd have to kill the next one.

She was wrong. He didn't enjoy this.

He *didn't*.

Ten

Rachael, a creature of instinct and, during certain times of the month, a creature of the moment who did not comprehend the concept of *tomorrow* or even *later,* would never be able to remember exactly how they'd ended up kissing.

They had been having a nice let's-get-acquainted chat. And then she was crying—and shocked! *Where did that come from? Has that been in me the whole time?* She didn't know if she should be appalled or sad or pleased or embarrassed.

Scratch that: she should be embarrassed. She *was* embarrassed.

Then Edward was there, frantically grabbing napkins and handing them to her as fast as he could while making soothing motions with his hands. She got to her feet and sort of stumbled toward the front of the store, and Edward got up and came after her so quickly he smashed his hip against a magazine display hard enough to make it rock.

"Rachael, it's okay. Don't leave, okay? Please? Come on, come back and sit down with me some more."

Anxiety. Concern. Lust.

Not pity, though. No, not that. And *he* wasn't embarrassed that a woman he'd just met was sobbing next to a display of *Time*, *Newsweek*, and *People* magazine's "Most Annoying People."

That was sort of nice. Sort of wonderful, really.

So she turned back toward him, turned to go back to their little corner table, and he reached for her—probably for her hand, but she would never know for certain—and she reached, too. And for a wonder, her hands were on his face, and his expression mirrored his scent. That was sort of wonderful, too. A lot of non-Pack said one thing while they thought another. Werewolves couldn't, which is why they tended to keep to themselves.

And then she was pulling him closer, and he was pulling her closer, and their mouths met. Softly at first, almost carefully, and then—

Lust. Concern. Happiness. Lust.

—they were holding each other and his kisses weren't soft anymore, and she was glad. She was not in a soft mood.

"Aw, jeez." From very, very far away, Rachael heard one of the clerks calling a manager. It sounded like he was hailing them from the bottom of a well. "Dave, could you get up here? I got another set of geeks making out in the paranormal romance section. And they are not stopping. Repeat, they are not stopping. Code Vlad, repeat, code Vlad!"

Which was how they earned a lifetime ban from Barnes and Noble.

Eleven

"Lifetime ban. A lifetime ban!" Edward was trying to wrap his mind around the astonishing events of the last twenty minutes. "But I'm a member of their discount club! They can't ban a member of their discount club, right?"

"They did, though."

Rachael's voice, low and sweet, also conveyed her extreme amusement. He was glad. Amused was good. Giving him a left cross in the front teeth because she felt molested was not.

And oh my God, her mouth tasted like a Green Tea Frappuccino. And SHE kissed ME!

"Listen, Rachael . . ." He reached for her small warm hand without thinking, realized what he was doing, and let his hand drop back to his side. "I wouldn't want you to get the idea that—"

"You troll bookstore shelves to pick up babes?" And for a wonder, *she* reached for *his* hand, and held it.

I will never wash this hand again, as Jabba is my witness. By all the gods in the Marvel universe, I will never . . . Pay attention, dumb shit! She's still talking!

"Woe to me, then, the latest victim of your Bookstore Nosh." She laughed. Rachael had a wonderful laugh, sort of deep and bubbly at the same time. It was a little strange to hear it when he could still see the tear tracks on her cheeks. "Perhaps you're *my* victim, Edward. Did you ever think of that?"

"I've *fantasized* about that," he admitted. He didn't want to. He absolutely did not. He wouldn't. Nope.

He peeked at his watch and groaned.

"You have to go." It wasn't a question.

"I kind of do."

Curse you, evil vampire queen who lives on Summit Avenue and is planning to enslave infants. The first awesome chick I meet in . . . what year was it? . . . the first awesome chick I meet in forever, and I have to ditch her to play I Spy with the undead. "But, Rachael, I swear this isn't some scam so I can make out with you and then head for the hills like a scalded rabbit, never to be seen again. I'd never do that, and anyone who *would* do that to someone like you should be strung up by his testicles with fishing line, but—"

"I know it isn't a scam." Her lips had curved into a smile at *fishing line.* "I know you truly need to be somewhere else, and truly hate it." And she gave him a smile of such sweet calm, he would have bought her a hundred Green Tea Frappuccinos.

"Right! Exactly! Duty calls. But I—"

"Want to see me again." Again: not a question. He couldn't recall being so comfortable, so soon, with anyone, never mind a super-hot brainy brunette.

"Anybody ever tell you how easy you are to talk to?"

"No."

"Oh. Because you are." *Asking a girl out never used to be this easy. Maybe being out of practice is improving my sex appeal. Or maybe she's got a fever.* "You really, really are."

"Many people would disagree."

"Morons," he said with no hesitation, and this time they both laughed. Then they were done with mirth and just looked at each other. He had to leave and he couldn't, so they stood on the sidewalk outside the "and stay out!" bookstore and looked and looked and looked.

It won't work. This is going too well. She's just being nice. Someone like that? Could have anybody. Anybody at all.

"We should see each other again very soon," she said, and he thought he was going to pitch a header into the sidewalk from sheer relief. Or into the storefront window; wouldn't *that* please the manager!

"Tomorrow morning?" he blurted. "Breakfast?"

She frowned, and faster than he would have believed, it felt like everything inside him had been flash frozen. "I've got to meet with a friend of the family . . . She thinks she's got some clients to send my way. A late lunch?"

I'll put off the stakeout until late afternoon again. How much trouble are a bunch of evil suckheads gonna get into during daylight hours, anyway?

"Late lunch," he agreed. "Where?"

She hesitated. "I don't really know the area. And you don't, either. Is there a place you want to try?"

"The Oceanaire," he said at once.

"Seafood?" Her adorable nose wrinkled in an adorable way, and she had an adorable-yet-perturbed expression on her adorable face. "In Minnesota?"

"You got this place all wrong," he assured her. "It's good stuff. You'll never think you have to go to Legal Sea Foods again."

"Ohhhh, Legals. Umm, did you ever have their Arctic char? Sublime. How do you know this? Research?"

"Sure. And you come across as a planner. You probably researched, too."

"Well, I rented *Fargo*." She laughed. "And I have to say, I loved the accent (and Frances McDormand). Midwestern accents sound so homey to me. Like when Paula Deen talks and I suddenly want her to start spooning mashed potatoes into my mouth. Can you hear it out here? The accent? They exaggerated it a bit in *Fargo*, you know . . ."

"I can hear yours," he said, smiling.

"Oh. Really? I have one?" She jerked a thumb at herself. "I *do*?"

"You drop the occasional *r*."

"You mean when I pahk the cah at Hahvahd Yahd?"

He shuddered. "I really hate it when people say that. A fake Boston accent is one of the worst sounds in the world. It's up there with Kanye West taking Taylor Swift's mike away."

"You've got a point. I didn't expect . . . I mean, I like some of the things I've seen out here."

Please be talking about me, please be talking about me, please be talking about me . . .

". . . place I'm staying turned out to be kind of terrific. Which made me ashamed. I've done nothing but find fault with the state of Minnesota since I showed up," she admitted. "I hear myself talking like a jerk . . ."

"And yet, make no effort to change," he teased.

"You shush. And you'd better go. You're late already, aren't you?"

"Dammit!" *Slammin' hot, super-smart, funny, hot, smart, and the most intuitive person I've ever met. God, if this is another one of your sick jokes, you and I are DONE, pal! You'll be off the Christmas list again!* "Of all the—dammit!"

"You didn't think we were going to stand out on this sidewalk all night, did you?"

Only in my dreams. "So tomorrow? Can I call you?"

"I'm planning on it, Edward. So you'd *better* call me. I am *no* fun at all when I've been disappointed."

"Right. Right! Okay. Okay, I'll see you tomorrow. But I'll talk to you earlier! Or leave you a voice mail." He wanted to kiss her again, but they really did only just meet, so he grabbed her hand and wrung it like a politician canvassing red states. "Great to meet you, Rachael. Soooo great! Okay." He ran to his rental car, screeched in mid-scamper, then turned around, abashed. "Um . . . Rachael . . ."

"Six, five, one. Two, six, one. Seven, four, four, four."

"Got it!" He waved, squashed the impulse to run back and kiss her ripe mouth some more, then hopped in his Rent-A-Prius and roared out of the parking lot.

The drive to the vampire queen's lair had never gone so quickly.

Twelve

Rachael walked into Cain's office, her nose in *Minnesota for Morons*. She hadn't meant to let the book capture her, but Cain had kept her waiting, so she had pulled it out and then . . . and then . . . and then Cain's assistant *really* hollered and Rachael realized Cain was ready for their meeting.

"You know," she said, engrossed, "Stillwater might be very nice. It's old, comparably speaking. And the river looks so pretty."

"Consider visiting. Now."

That got her head up in a hurry. *Anger. Fear. Anxiety.*

She snapped the book closed. "What's wrong?"

Cain was behind her desk, pinching the bridge of her nose. She looked like she hadn't changed her clothes in three days. She, ah, smelled like it, too.

"A public relations nightmare. That is what's wrong." Cain stopped pinching and looked up. "I'm sorry. There have been some murders."

"Local?"

"Yes."

"Pack?"

Cain blanched. "Good God, I don't think so. That's *all* we need, dead Pack members popping up right when the Pack leader's cousin gets to town. Michael would be so pleased."

Rachael snorted. *Pleased* wasn't the word that leapt to her mind when wondering about Michael Wyndham's reaction to a Pack murder spree. *What constitutes a spree, anyway? She said* murders, *plural. Two? Is two a spree?*

"You're jammed," she guessed.

"Extremely."

"You could have called . . . we didn't have to meet today."

"We did have to meet today, Rachael. I'm sorry to have to tell you . . . this is going to sound a little odd, but the two victims were on a list of small business owners who are looking for an accountant." Cain coughed. "A list I had drawn up for you and was prepared to give to you this morning." Cain slid the list across her desk. "I strongly advise you not waste your time calling Mr. Stewart or Ms. Janesboro."

Less than a week?

A WEEK?

Cuz, you are in for the spanking of your life if I ever get back to the Cape.

"And we don't validate parking." Rachael had been using the parking stub for a bookmark. "Sorry."

A never-ending nightmare.

Thirteen

Edward nearly drove into the pillar in the underground parking garage (it came out of nowhere!), so he stomped the brake and tried to calm down. *You can't meet up with Rachael if you're found mangled in the Hilton parking garage with the front of your car squashed in like an accordion. So get a grip, shithead!*

He tried to calm down, but wonder of wonders, a space right next to the elevators had just opened up (it was possible the driver saw him racing into the garage and narrowly missing a fiery death, and got the hell out), so he pounced on it. Then he glanced in the rearview mirror, tried (and failed) to straighten his messy bangs, popped a breath mint, and then shoved his shoulder against the door so hard it went immediately numb.

Moron! You have to OPEN the car door to get out!

Right.

So he did.

On the elevator leading to street level, he tortured himself with the most likely scenarios. 1) Rachael had been a hologram. 2) Rachael got off on stringing geeks along and had no plans to see him again, ever. 3) Rachael had been run down like a squirrel in a senseless pedestrian vs. dirt bike collision. 4) Rachael had been too nice to say no to his face, so she said yes while having no intention of meeting him. 5) Rachael was a robot.

He had agonized over what to wear. He had no idea how long he would be spying for Boo, and he hated shopping even more than packing, so he hadn't brought much more than a suitcase full of clothes. Rattled and wearing nothing but his Homer Simpson boxers, he called Gregory.

"Whoa, whoa, slow down. You . . . wait. You have a date?"

"Yeah."

"*You* do."

"Yeah."

"But you haven't even been out there a week."

"Did I call you for a timeline? No, Gregory, I didn't. And if I wanted someone to shatter my dating self-esteem I would have called Boo's cell. So, nice restaurant. Seafood restaurant in downtown Minneapolis."

"You're calling me while you're wearing your Simpsons underpants, aren't you?"

"Dude, do you really want me to answer? Because I will.

And nobody says *underpants* anymore. And if you don't help me, I'll take a picture of Homer and me and send it to your phone about fifty times. A day!"

It wasn't easy to threaten or cow a vampire, but Edward thought it had gone nicely. He was wearing tan slacks, a light blue dress shirt, and his leather jacket. Loafers, with his lucky Yoda socks.

Thank God I splurged on the extra-strength deodorant.

He stepped out of the elevator, took a moment to get his bearings, and then spotted her chatting with the hostess by the entrance. "Oh thank God, thank God," he murmured to himself.

Rachael turned, almost like she'd heard him (which she couldn't; too much background noise), and smiled. She had a great smile. And a wonderful dentist; he'd never seen teeth so straight and white.

"Did you think I wasn't going to come?" she asked as he galloped to her side. "Shame, shame."

"Well, you did seem a little too good to be true," he admitted.

"I'd never stand you up. I know what it's like and I'd never do it. Not even to someone I didn't want to get to know."

He stared at her. "What colossal dumb shit bailed on a date with *you*? And did you suggest they get sterilized so they don't muck up the gene pool any worse than it is? Because the thought of someone that dumb just roaming the earth at will is terrifying."

"Eugenics never came up," she said dryly. "Besides, it was never going to work. At times, I've got a terrible temper."

"You?" Had she even raised her voice yet? "You seem pretty laid back." No. That wasn't quite right. Calm, maybe. And not easily spooked, or excited. "Hard to imagine you hulking out."

"It does happen on occasion." She tipped him a wink. "Why, I've been known to *eat* men who stand me up."

He stared again. And again. The hostess was talking to him. Why was the hostess bugging him? Was she taking a restaurant survey? Why wouldn't she leave them alone? Was she canvassing for UNICEF? Time and place, lady, time and place. Jesus!

"Do you have a reservation, sir?"

Sure. He was positive. Absolutely they had a reservation. Table for two. Yep. Now if he could only remember his last name . . .

Eureka! "Batley, table for two, please."

"You've got to stop this," Rachael mock-scolded. "You're going to turn my head with all the lovely attention."

He was very, *very* tempted to kiss her for that statement alone. It seemed amazing but true: Rachael-the-goddess found flop sweat, the shakes, major horniness, and anxiety endearing.

She'd turned and followed the hostess, and he in turn followed Rachael. He tried, tried—*tried*—to be a gentleman, but she was just too slammin'. Nope, slammin' didn't do her justice: she was slammin' squared. No, cubed!

She was wearing one of those dresses that looked like a big

long shirt, in greenish blue, no stockings. Her rich brown hair hung at shoulder length, with a kind of ripple through it, not quite a curl. Some kind of black shoes. What did women call shoes that weren't high heels? Anyway, she was wearing black shoes that weren't high heels.

Then they were being seated and examining the menu. "Hmmmm. This is not bad at all. What are you thinking?"

"That it's so great to see you," he replied fervently.

She smiled. "What are you thinking of ordering?"

"Oh." He immediately felt like a horse's ass, but Rachael didn't seem to mind (again!). "Uh . . ." He was so keyed up, he figured everything would taste like wet napkins no matter what he ordered, so he just asked for a bowl of clam chowder.

"Cheap date," she teased.

"Yeah, but it's my date. I asked you out." *After a little prompting*, he reminded himself. "It's my treat, Rachael, honest. Please order whatever you want."

"Priiicey. Though I think *that's* a wonderful touch." She pointed and he turned. Dozens of FedEx shipping labels were taped over the oyster bar, proving the seafood in question hadn't been on the premises longer than forty-eight hours.

"It is, huh? Guess that's why they gouge us. Ten bucks for asparagus, nine bucks for mushrooms . . ."

"What?"

"Okay, I might have seen a flash of the temper you were talking about earlier because you said that really, really loudly."

"Nine bucks? The lobster I understand. The clam chowder I—Jesus! Forty bucks for halibut? Do we get to adopt it and take it home and raise it and send it to an Ivy League college?" She glared as the waitress bounced up to the table, all smiles and sleek hair and neatly pressed pants and apron. "We're from Boston. Boston! And you're way overcharging us." She turned back to him. "Edward, you don't have to pay, truly. Please let me treat you."

"No way. I'm loaded, baby. I'm a rich retiree. Can't you tell?"

"The Yoda socks gave it away," she replied, rolling her eyes. He was astounded. Rachael had, among her many, many, many attributes, a fine eye for detail.

"Did you have any questions about our menu, miss?"

"Sooooo many questions. How does your boss sleep at night, that would be question number one. And can I get the scallops without the tortilla chips? That would be question number two." Then she coughed, and he could swear she seemed ashamed, or embarrassed. "And I'm sorry about greeting you like I did. I'm homesick and I'm being quite the bitch about it."

"Rachael! Nuh-uh!"

"Don't listen to him," she told the bemused waitress. "He's madly in lust. But I do apologize. Although I have to warn you, all the food you bring us had better be spectacular."

"Don't make her angry. You wouldn't like her when she's angry."

"You shush."

They ordered, the waitress left, and when Rachael gave him the full force of her dark gaze, he knew that if he never saw her again after that night, he would always, always think of her.

"A retired man of leisure . . . how nice for you. What are you, really?"

Good question. Sidekick? Besotted date? IT guy? Tourist? Vamp stalker? All of the above? None of the above?

"I took a leave of absence from Grate and Tate—"

"Not the Boston firm!"

"Uh, yeah." He mentally braced himself for, *Oh. You're an accountant? Um. How exciting. No, really. Um, I think the diarrhea's coming back so let's just hang it up for tonight, okay?*

"I'm an accountant, too!"

He instantly rewrote the dialogue in his head: *I think accountants are the hottest thing on the planet! I continually fantasize about being spanked by an accountant! I wish you would spank me while filing my tax return! Mmmm . . . Mama likey . . .*

"Are you all right?" she asked.

Go away, boner! No one hit your buzzer. "Oh, fine. I'm fine."

"You're between jobs?" she asked with genuine interest (he was pretty sure).

"No, but I've been working since I was sixteen, Grate and Tate pay well and have super bennies, and I have no life, so I've got five figures in savings. I was able to take a leave of absence."

"Hard to believe."

"I'm frugal, baby."

"I meant about having no life. You seem quite lively to *me*," she teased.

He could feel the blood rush to his face. "Thanks." Then he cleared his throat to try to cover for his hot face and said, "So what are you gonna get?"

"Laid, I hope," she said, and that was when he spilled his water all over himself.

Fourteen

He was fumbling with the key card and dropped it and she snatched it up and then she dropped it (most likely because his hands were pretty busy under her dress) and somehow they managed to get the damned hotel room unlocked and fell inside.

His hands were everywhere, his mouth was on hers; he was groaning and so was she. She yanked and heard his pants rip. *Careful. Careful.*

So far, quite the successful first date. *Hmm. I guess I'm that kind of girl now. The kind who ruthlessly seduces on a first date. Edward never had a chance . . . not that he seems to mind.*

No, he didn't seem to mind.

They had spent the evening gorging on the most overpriced seafood she'd ever had, and it was worth every penny.

The halibut: buttery and tender and flaky. His chowder (which he kindly let her taste and, when she liked it, he insisted she finish his bowl while he ordered another for himself): thick and creamy and studded with plump clams. Her seafood tower (yes! A seafood *tower*, what a wonderful thing!): shrimp so perfectly chilled they were bursting with plump meaty flavor, clams and mussels so fresh she could smell the ocean on them. Her second order of raw oysters: sweet and briny and luscious at the same time, and well over a dozen went down her throat.

And all the while, they played the seduction game.

"You're still using the Sage program?" Edward asked, incredulous. "Do you drive around in a covered wagon, too?"

"It's perfect for my needs," she insisted. "You won't get me to back down this time, Edward. Though I grudgingly admit you were right about the updates—keeping track of the fundraising can be difficult without it. But I need something that'll serve organizations of different sizes. Besides, Sage is compatible with Windows *and* Linux *and* Unix."

"But it—"

"Plus I need to manage finances for all sorts of locations; I did that back on the Cape and I want to continue doing it out here." Snatch clam. Hold to mouth. Tilt head back. Slurp.

"Yeah, but—"

"Sorry to cut you off again, but I don't want to get locked into *only* taking small business owners or *only* taking government work or *only* taking nonprofits." She shook her empty clam at him. "That's why it's perfect for me."

"What about overseas?"

"What *about* overseas?" She picked up another clam and sucked it down.

"That's why you need the Epicor."

"No."

"Yes."

"You do not have Epicor."

"I *absolutely* have Epicor, and the thing is a demigod as far as I'm concerned, okay?" Edward was on his second bowl of chowder, she was glad to see. His appetite was getting stronger the more they talked.

So was hers. But not for food.

She liked how he had obviously taken some care with his wardrobe. She liked how clean he smelled. She liked his insistence on defending his workplace tools of choice. She liked his excitement and his passion and his manners. She even liked that he would not budge on the topic of who would pay for lunch.

But she had a way to make that up to him, maybe. She could insist on a second date. Or she could . . .

"I don't believe it."

He smirked. "Jealousy . . . tsk, tsk, Rachael."

"No, I'll admit it, that's impressive. It really does everything they say?"

"It practically cooks me breakfast."

"Maybe you'll show me sometime?"

"Maybe I'll show you whatever you want anytime."

"Ah, now that's a pledge I will hold you to."

"Good! And my God." He was staring at the litter of empty shells, the stack growing ever higher. But he was smiling, and even if he hadn't been, she would know he was pleased. "You can really put it away."

"No worries; I'm still saving room for dessert. Baked Alaska! As long as we're obliged to spend so much money this evening, I see no use in half measures."

"My kind of woman. Listen, you will lose your mind when you see how it handles Cloud solutions."

"Oh my God."

"Not to mention customers in, what, one hundred fifty countries?"

Now it was her turn to stare. "That's amazing. I've always wanted to stretch, but I run a one-woman op."

"And cheap, for what you get."

She seized his hand, quicker and faster than she meant to, and let go when he yelped. "Sorry. Tell me more. Talk to me about supply chain management."

So he did. And then she started to shake. She managed to force "When?" through her teeth.

"Uh . . ." He was staring again, which she didn't mind a bit. *Lust. Interest. Lust.* "I can show you on my laptop—"

"When can we get out of here?"

Lust. Lust. Confusion. Excitement. "You're not talking about my laptop, are you?"

The oyster shell she was holding suddenly broke in several pieces; in her excitement she'd squeezed too hard. "No. I'm talking about going to your place or mine and getting naked and spending the rest of the evening trying to hurt each other in various ways, with possible breaks for long showers, and maybe toast, after." Something about discussing the latest software advancements in her field did it to her every time . . .

"You. Are. My. Hero." He looked around and screamed, "Waitress!"

Fifteen

As it happened, neither of them wanted to waste time driving to his hotel room or her temporary apartment, which is how they ended up on the floor of room 217 in the Minneapolis Hilton, just upstairs from the restaurant.

Rachael had been between boyfriends for nearly two years, and she suspected Edward had been deprived of sex as well. *That sort of thing can't be good for us*, she mused as he tried to unbutton her shirt dress with trembling fingers.

In this case, it was a good thing, a wonderful thing, because his black excitement merely kindled her own. Which is why they never made it to the bed, only four feet from where they were lying.

He tugged and pulled and she tried to help while their

mouths fought and tasted each other, but really all they did was get in each other's way, until . . .

"Fuck it," he growled in a voice so deep she could barely make out what he'd said. Then he tugged, hard, and buttons went flying and his hands were on her bra, over her bra, under her bra, and then her bra was up to her neck and she didn't care at all.

She didn't care that much of his weight was on her, either. She kind of liked it. She knew he couldn't help it, that he was operating through a fog of lust so thick he probably couldn't remember either of their names. Strange, though. Usually she disliked that behavior, being squashed beneath a laboring man . . . male werewolves tended toward being control freaks during sex. It was all about domination. Not that she minded a bit of domination now and again—it was good for the digestion if nothing else—but she liked how it didn't feel like a contest with Edward.

They both wanted exactly the same thing. And they were both determined to get it.

She reached down, found his belt buckle, yanked. It came loose with terrific ease and she flung it away, and then her fingers were busy at his zipper and he groaned into her mouth.

She wriggled beneath him, trying to help him when she felt his hands on the backs of her thighs, lifting her toward him. She managed to tug her panties down enough to let him in, then seized his warm, sweetly throbbing member. She started to guide it inside her as he surged forward. Then she brought her knees up and pulled him to her as he sucked on her lower lip and thrust.

And oh God, it was everything, it was the world, *he* was the world. "Ah!"

He stopped at once and she could feel the tension in his arms, the muscles thrumming as he fought not to slam into her again, fought despite the way his body was screaming his need to both of them. "Ah, shit, I'm sorry, Rachael. Did I hurt you?"

"Yes. And you'd better do it again or you'll need to find a dentist immediately."

He laughed into her mouth and surged forward again, and she—

lust lust lust lust lust lust lust lust lust lust lust lust lust lust lust lust lust lust lust lust lust lust lust lust lust lust lust lust lust lust lust lust lust lust lust lust lust lust lust lust lust lust lust lust lust lust lust lust lust lust lust lust lust lust lust lust lust lust lust lust lust lust

—wasn't quite sure where her desires ended and his began, and didn't much care, either.

She met him at every stroke and (*very* unusual for her!) felt her climax start to build almost at once, felt the familiar-yet-strange sensation of an orgasm bearing down on her like a fighter jet.

Yes, it's definitely been too long. Far, far too long, and my God, Edward! Where has your dick been all my life?

"Ah, God," she groaned. "I'm going to come, Edward, sorry, I'm going—ahhhhh!"

His teeth had been nibbling the hollow of her throat, his hands were fisted in her hair, and he ground out something like, "Thhkkk ddd," which she assumed was "Thank God."

She knew why, could feel the muscles in his body actually shift as he reached his own point of no return. Then he was stiffening in her arms, went rigid in her arms. She could feel the new rush of heat inside her, saw his eyes roll up, and thought, *Good thing we're on the floor; I don't think either of us could have kept our feet.*

Then he collapsed over her, whispering, "Oh my God, oh my God, oh my God, oh my God."

Her thoughts exactly.

Sixteen

"Oh, my." She traced her finger over the fresh, orange-sized bruise he had on his left hip. "Did you forget to wear your safety equipment?"

"After what just happened, I should definitely get some," he agreed.

His hair was adoringly rumpled. (Adoringly? Hair can be *adoringly* rumpled? If she had heard some other ninny say it, she would have laughed herself sick.)

He glanced down and saw the bruise she was gently stroking. "Oh, that. Yeah. When you had your crying jag in the Starbucks at Barnes—"

"It was not a jag."

"I got up to go with you and knocked into one of those big old display cases."

"Ouch." She took a closer look; it was closer to grapefruit-sized than orange-sized. "That must have hurt." She had great respect for injuries suffered by those not of the Pack. How could they tolerate days and days of healing? Wasn't it maddening? Agony? The continual pain, the way the marks took so long to go away, the incapacitation . . . and they had to eat *medicine*! If it was a terrible injury, they had to eat medicine or they would get an infection and *die*. Infection sounded like a terrible thing. She didn't know how they tolerated it. "Do you need a doctor?"

"For that?" He laughed, a cheerful, sunny sound. Strange to associate *sunny* with Edward when right now, at close to midnight, it was anything but. "Jeez, Rachael, I'm a severe wimp, but not that big a wimp."

She sat up so abruptly he nearly went sprawling. "Who called you that? Where are they?" She glanced around the dark room as if looking for the insensitive bullying moron who *dared* . . . who would actually call someone so wonderful . . . call them a . . .

"I called me that. Whoa, calm down. What? Didn't bother me any. You should see my friend Boo. Did you ever see *Zombieland*?"

She shook her head. She liked the way he was staring at her breasts while speaking casually. She liked the way she could smell his desire flare up when seconds earlier it had been barely banked coals.

"No? Deprived woman! Okay, we'll Netflix it. I haven't unpacked all my DVDs yet. Anyway, there's a character in *Zombieland*, Tallahassee, and he's described as a guy who 'sets the standard for not to be fucked with.' That's my friend Boo."

"Hard to imagine ferocity from someone named Boo."

"That's the trick, y'see. Nobody ever sees her coming. She likes it like that."

She started to ask if she would meet his friend, then thought, *Why would I? We've only just met. We have lives waiting for us in Massachusetts. We probably won't see each other much now that we've scratched our itch.*

Then she thought, *We reside in the same area now, and when we go back to our lives, we'll also live near each other. Does it mean something?*

She shoved the thoughts away—long-term relationship planning was not generally a Pack strength unless a pregnancy was involved. The imperative to start and raise a family was strong, even more so than for humans. "And you?" She was trailing her fingers from the bruise, across his stomach, up his ribs . . . "What do you like?"

"Uh . . ."

Over his nipples, back down his stomach, following his dark blond treasure trail (a description she had always found silly but apt), down into the thatch at his groin.

"Edward?"

"Sorry, I can't hear you over the rush of blood in my ears."
He shook his head as if to clear it and she laughed again. She
couldn't remember the last time she'd laughed so much, or been
so physically satisfied. "The harder I get, the more I can actually sense my IQ dropping. It's kind of cool and terrifying at
the same time."

But how satisfied was she, how sated, if she was ready to go
back for seconds? If they both were?

Maybe it's about more than scratching an itch.

And maybe not. "Ah, the trials and tribulations of walking
around with a penis."

"I know! You have no idea what we menfolk endure."

Maybe he's your mate. Oh, now there was a silly thought.
They barely knew each other. And yes, other Pack members
occasionally took non-Pack to mate, but it was rare. And
Edward . . . they'd eat him alive, so to speak, if she brought
him home.

Maybe this is home now.

*It isn't! This was never meant to be a permanent living situation!
I have a life, a job, family to return to. Anything else—everything
else—is just a distraction.*

She forced a smile. "You're not fooling me, you know."

"Huh?" His voice was getting thick with desire.

"I know you want me."

This time he was the one to laugh, and she loved how his

joy affected the urgent tang to his scent, like strawberries and balsamic vinegar. You'd never think the two would pair well, but the result was surprisingly strong.

And sweet.

"What gave it away? When earlier I said, 'Oh my God, oh my God, you're so wet' or when I applied my penis to your—"

"Oh, God. Please stop that." She covered her face. "Applied? Don't ever say *applied* when discussing mating."

"Don't do that." He gently grabbed her wrists and pulled them away. "You're way, way too gorgeous to ever cover that face."

"That's irrelevant." And it was. She had no power over how she looked. It seemed silly to get credit for something she had nothing to do with.

"Don't you know, Rachael? Didn't anybody tell you? You're so beautiful." He stroked his thumb across her right eyebrow and tucked a strand of hair behind her ear. "You're just so beautiful."

"Irrelevant," she said again, feeling the blood climb into her face. *Blushing like a ninny, very attractive. Next you'll swoon.* "But you're sweet to say so."

"In your lexicon, *sweet* translates to *stud*, right?"

"Oh, yes."

"Called it! And I'm standing by my implication that figuring out you're making me massively horny doesn't exactly qualify you for Mensa."

"Just for that," she teased, "no oral sex for you."

"Noooooooooo!" He had shaken his fists at the ceiling, startling the shit out of her. "Like that? That's my Darth Vader *nooooo!* and did you notice that I did it a hundred times better than stupid Hayden Christensen? Hey, I wanted the guy to do well, okay? I wanted him to nail it. But he just—"

"Please stop talking about Darth Vader and fuck me."

"Wow. Torn between two lovers. On the one hand—yeeek! Oh, you're gonna pay for that one."

"I hope so."

Seventeen

They utterly abandoned their transplanted lives for the next fifty hours. They didn't leave their room, not once. And room service was kept busy, hopping back and forth with late suppers, with late breakfasts. With hot fudge sundaes at midnight, with shrimp cocktails (she ate them like dessert . . . they were so plump and sweet!), with toothbrushes and toothpaste, and with various other essentials neither of them had brought. Rachael put the whole thing on her Amex; she refused to let Edward drop one cent.

They explored the shower, they explored the living room in their small suite, they explored each other. They told each other stories about themselves, and they watched several in-room movies, including the new X-Men, the new Hulk ("It's

MaryJanice Davidson

the third remake!" Edward exclaimed, sucking down his second sundae), and the old *Zombieland*. And Rachael agreed with Edward's assessment of the character Tallahassee: he definitely set "the standard for not to be fucked with." In fact, she privately thought he could almost be Pack in the way he focused on fights and never worried about tomorrow.

But all good things must end. And there were the dead people to wonder about.

She hadn't realized it, but she had been subconsciously worrying about the problem of the recent murders, people who might have been her new clients but for meeting up with the wrong person. She doubted it was a coincidence, but now began to wonder if it wasn't a deliberate attempt to sow discord among either the vampires or the Pack.

Or the vampires *and* the Pack.

So she needed to do something she had thought to avoid for at least a month. She needed a face-to-fang with the vampire queen.

Fortunately, Edward was as ready to go back to his temporary life as she was, if for no other reason than to get clean clothes. They shared a long, hot, wet good-bye kiss at the door to their room, and at the doors to the elevator, and down the elevator, and in the lobby, and in the parking garage. The parking garage was the best, because he'd leaned her against a car and began doing the most delicious things with his—

"If I wake up in my dumb hotel bed and find out this whole

thing was the wet dream of champions, I'm gonna be super-pissed," was his tender farewell. They promised to get together again as soon as they could. They promised to call and text to shorten the time between seeing each other. They promised to be careful and to talk soon.

But one of them was lying.

Eighteen

Mrs. Cain looked, if anything, more haggard than she had when Rachael had last seen her. So she greeted her with, "Not another murder?"

"No, thank all the gods. But it's wreaking havoc on our new ad campaign. 'Come to Minnesota . . . and be killed!'"

"It's not as good as 'Florida is for lovers,'" Rachael agreed.

"I'm afraid I have no new information for you, other than the fact that the victims were most definitely not Pack."

"Or, presumably, vampire."

Mrs. Cain blinked. "No. Of course not. But can you imagine? How would they ever cover it up?"

"No idea. But about the victims being vanilla humans, I

figured. I stopped by to let you know I'm off to set up a meeting with the vampire queen."

"You're what?" Mrs. Cain had surged to her feet so quickly only another Pack member could have tracked the movement. "Have you lost your mind?"

"Almost certainly not." *Except when it came to seducing a fellow accountant and watching* Zombieland *twice in a row, not to mention the french fry fight.* "I've been thinking since we last met, and I don't like this at all."

"I can assure you, you're not alone. No one likes it." She eased back down in her seat, looking past Rachael instead of at her. Typical Pack behavior: she was physically backing down so Rachael wouldn't assume the woman was challenging her. Although normally the domain of males, there were alpha and beta females as well, and, occasionally, Challenges. "But I fail to see what meeting with that woman would accomplish."

"I'm not sure, either, but think about it."

"I have been," she said, looking glum. "I've mentioned I don't like it, yes?"

So she wouldn't be seen as looming over the woman, Rachael plopped into a chair across from her. "Michael sends me to town to keep an eye on the queen, correct? And I'm no sooner here than people start turning up dead . . . people you had arranged for me to meet. That in itself is plenty odd, but what if someone is trying to stir up trouble between the vamps or the Pack?"

"I'm not—"

Rachael stepped on the woman's words. "What if someone is trying to stir up trouble between the vamps *and* our Pack? The situation is already awkward—many of our people haven't forgiven the vampire for letting our Antonia die in her service.

"And you can't tell me the vampires didn't resent having to show up in Massachusetts for what was essentially a trial for, at worst, murder, and at best, negligence. We parted on general good terms, but for a while it looked like we wouldn't. And it doesn't take but one spark to rekindle a blaze."

"I see what you're saying," she said slowly, her expression thoughtful. "Still. Very dangerous, I think."

"I agree. But nevertheless." She shrugged. If she hadn't been willing to get dirty, she never would have gotten on the plane. "Onward and upward, rah-rah-rah."

"No." Cain shook her head, her expression doubtful. "No, I think the risks are too high, Rachael. I think you'd better steer clear for now."

Rachael looked at the woman, whose fatigue was evident in every line on her broad, sad face. *When had she last slept? Poor lady; she's carrying weight that by rights is for others to tow.* So when she answered, she tried to do so as tactfully as possible.

"You misunderstand me, Mrs. Cain. I didn't come for permission. I came as a courtesy to your office . . . your *true* office, not the chamber."

Cain opened her mouth, but when Rachael held up a hand, she said nothing.

"I have acknowledged this as your territory, and I would never dream of trying for anything that's yours. But I also have permission from Michael, my cousin and *our Pack leader*, to proceed however I see fit. He did not tell me to avoid the queen; he did not tell me to engage the queen. He left the specifics entirely up to me. Seeing her, not seeing her, telling you or not telling you . . . all are my prerogative.

"Perhaps I wasn't clear. Perhaps it's my fault that you mistook courtesy for subservience. If that's so, I apologize and will try to be more clear in the future. Do you understand?"

Anger. Frustration. Shame. Fear. "I . . . see. Yes. I apologize; I only tried to convey concern for your safety. How could I face Michael if anything happened to you here?"

"We grew up together," she replied, smiling a little. She was relieved there wouldn't be an escalation. She supposed she wasn't very brave. There were plenty of females who would have loved to get bloody over something so minor. "He would know my grisly demise came through no fault of yours."

The older woman snorted. "Excellent point. And, if I may, if you're wondering about coincidences, have you considered the timing?"

She had. "The full moon."

"Two days away," Cain agreed. "Perhaps our killer is trying

to spook the vampires into going after a Pack member during the full moon."

"Lovely. Well, I'd better get going."

"How are you . . . I mean, if you don't mind, what are you going to say?"

"I have no idea, but I still think it's worth the risk. It's almost a win-win: if she's in on it, she'll at least know she's not operating in a vacuum, that people have noticed. If she's not in on it, she'll appreciate the warning and we'll maybe cement a little goodwill. The gain outweighs the risks." *A little. Probably.* But it was no time to show uncertainty. "Trust me. It will be fine."

Cain arched dark brows. "You hope."

"Yeah." Rachael sighed. "I hope." Then: "You *really* don't validate parking?"

Nineteen

The dead man walked out the front door, stood on the walk for a moment, then slowly ambled toward the street.

Edward, who had been daydreaming about Rachael, specifically Rachael's awesome boobs and wicked smile, was at first startled, then curious.

He'd come for another stakeout, but more out of guilt than any sense of urgency or duty. He hadn't been near the Manse O' the Undead in two days.

Oh, but what a two days!

She's perfect. She's a goddess. So smart, and so hot! And Jesus, her mouth. Sharp and sweet and urgent and ah, God, this is no time for another damn boner!

So he'd walked the neighborhood yet again, this time dressed like a tourist in black cotton shorts, a bright yellow polo shirt, and a black fanny pack, which, he was surprised to see in the mirror, made him look like a giant deranged bee. He tended to choose clothing the way he chose snacks: whatever was closest at hand is what he grabbed. Thus: the return of . . . Bee Man!

Look! Up in the sky! It's a bird, it's a plane, it's . . . gross. A giant bug.

He did look like a tourist, at least—he ought to know how to pull that off, given where he lived. Which was good, because if he was challenged, he'd ask for directions to the St. Paul Cathedral, which (per Google) was a few blocks from here.

Rachael really is astounding in every way, he thought, feeling a sappy smile spread across his face. *And a goddamned hurricane in bed. Best of my life. No question; absolute best. And not because of what she did with her hands and mouth. Because of the things she told me. Because she cried and didn't mind that I tried to help her. Because she admitted to being bitchy and homesick and could laugh at herself. Because she apologized to a waitress she'd never seen before and might never see again.*

And let's not forget the things she asked me to do to her. The naked things and the—

And here came the dead man. Not that Edward knew it then; he recognized the man as the same one who'd escorted the pregnant lady out . . . the scrubs helped. House call, maybe? Cigarette break? He wasn't doing much, just sort of wandering in the yard.

I'll get close. I'll get as good a look at him as I can. Maybe he's not an evil OB. Maybe he's a regular OB, hold the evil. Maybe . . . he's a prisoner. Maybe he needs help. I won't know if I don't get close. If he's a good guy, this might be his one chance at safety. I'm not gonna blow it for him because I don't want to get spotted.

Summit Avenue was utterly quiet as twilight deepened. Edward decided getting closer was worth the risk. So he swallowed his nervousness as best he could and, as casually as he could, started walking across the street. When he got close to the fence, he waved.

Nothing wrong here, just another dumb tourist who didn't bother with MapQuest . . . Nothing to worry about . . . certainly not someone spying on you or possibly someone you live with . . .

"Hey! Excuse me . . . I'm sorry to bother you, but I think I'm lost."

"I think you are, too."

The friendly hey-I'm-a-hapless-tourist smile fell off his face. Edward had gotten close enough to realize he was talking to a dead man.

Not a prisoner on death row.

Not a vampire.

A dead man.

He was so startled he tripped on the curb and fell, flailing, to the sidewalk. He caught himself by the hands, but not quite fast enough.

What a stupid way to meet my first-ever zombie, he thought, clutching his skinned knees and trying not to groan with humiliation and pain.

Twenty

The zombie was pretty helpful.

"That looks like it stings," it told him. It had hurried (sort of) through the gate and helped him up off the sidewalk. Edward braced himself for utter revulsion, but the zombie's grip was surprisingly free of grossness. It was cool, but firm. Nothing squished. Nothing oozed onto his own hand.

He was able to get a good look at the zombie and, now that his shock was receding, was almost disappointed. The zombie was cool to the touch, yes, but not gross; it wasn't teeming with maggots and wasn't shuffling toward him moaning, "Braaaaaaains."

Kind of a letdown, really.

Welcome to my life, zombie. Things are never as cool as they are in the movies.

"I'm a doctor," the zombie was telling him, just when he thought things couldn't get any weirder. Oh, of course. A *doctor* zombie made perfect sense. Yep.

It continued in a voice that sounded helpful, if a little hoarse. From disuse? From slowly rotting vocal cords? "My name's Marc. D'you want to come in the house? I could get that cleaned up for yo—"

"No!" God, no. Never. He was no match for vampires and zombies and, if the rumors were true, ghosts. *No* match. "It's fine, it's just a scrape, I—I—" He forced himself to take a breath. "Are *you* all right? You look . . ." Dead. Defeated. Dead. And also, dead. ". . . pale," he finished.

"Oh. Well." It shrugged one shoulder. "I've been sick."

I'll bet you have. For a moment, Edward was afraid he was going to giggle. If he did, he wouldn't stop. He wouldn't stop until somebody hit him a few times with a brick. And that would be bad.

And he still couldn't get over how a real-life zombie was nothing, nothing at all like the movies. It didn't stink, and it wasn't dressed in rotting rags. It had no visible marks or injuries. *Maybe he died of a drug overdose? He sure didn't get smashed by a car or fall off some scaffolding.* Its eyes were clear, not clouded with death, though the corneas weren't as bluish as they could have been.

No, what gave the zombie away—

Marc, the zombie's name is Marc.

—was how it could stand so still. The lack of animation in body and facial expression, the way it stood there like its batteries had run out (*which I guess they had*) was just unsettling enough to raise his hackles.

Here came the big question: what was a zombie doing here at all?

Then he remembered the pregnant woman and felt the chill that came from knowing something awful and realizing there wasn't much to be done to prevent the awful thing from happening.

Boo.

He had to call Boo. *Now.*

"Sorry to trouble you. I gotta get going. I'm late," he said, and then turned on his heel and began to sprint.

"Be careful," Marc-the-zombie called after him, which put the final surreal touch on the conversation.

If anyone had told me hanging around Summit Avenue in Minnesota would be way more exciting than vamp hunting in Boston with Boo, I would have suggested they up their meds.

Twenty-one

Rachael stopped by her apartment pro tem on the way to the queen's mansion. She did so partly because she wanted to make sure Edward hadn't left any messages for her, and partly because she was becoming quite fond of her den. Apartment. All right: den.

Well within walking distance of the queen's hideout, her apartment was part of the basement of a small Victorian, a two-story house with five bedrooms, nearly as many bathrooms, and a turret (a *turret*!). There was no yard to speak of, but Rachael was used to that from her years in the Boston area. Besides, there was a turret. (A *turret*!) It looked like they were smuggling princesses up there.

She parked her rental car in . . . no. She parked *the* rental car in the alley behind her apartment. No. *The* apartment.

Dammit, this was a temporary living situation, so: *The* rental car. *The* apartment.

Anyway. She parked in the alley behind the apartment, circled around to the front, and bounded up the steps. The porch floor was painted sky blue, and various sherbet-colored chairs from the sixties—clunky lawn chairs, which were bulky and made of too much metal—were scattered along the sizeable porch.

Well used to the Cape's orderly color schemes of cream and white and green and cream and white and cream, and sometimes green, and maybe red if the neighborhood was spiraling out of control, the odd pastel colors more than pleased her. She found them delightful.

Perhaps the Cape could stand with some color changes; perhaps if they tried something more daring and less conventional . . . ack! Traitorous thought!

She opened the front door, realizing (again) that it hadn't been locked and remembering (again) that it never was, until her landlord went to bed.

All right. She would confess. That was something she could get used to, and no lie.

The entryway was all dark blond wood and hardwood floors waxed to a high gloss. The stairs were much the same—the house smelled more of floor wax and cleaning supplies than anything else. Given how old it was, Rachael was beyond grateful. More than once she'd walked into a Cape Cod cottage that reeked of dead fish and dust.

If she took the stairs up, she'd find herself in the area of the house the landlord shared with his elderly wife and their grown son. Their grown son lived in the turret, fortunate bastard.

They were all human, which she had expected. Humans outnumbered Pack by a minimum of fifty to one. She'd been fortunate Mrs. Cain was in the Midwest, and in a position of power to help a Pack member newly come to Minnesota's capital.

She took the stairs down and down (there were quite a few). The more she burrowed, the calmer she felt, until she was standing in her small living room.

Mrs. Cain hadn't known (as Rachael herself had not) how long she would be staying, so she'd rented a furnished apartment. The small basement area was decorated with several rugs in jewel colors, while the walls were lined with cement blocks of a color she had never before seen: rose. They were, she had to admit, the most glamorous cement bricks she had ever seen. She hadn't been aware bricks *came* in rose. There was an old-fashioned rolltop desk that gave off a strong, though not unpleasant, odor of decades of furniture polish.

The worst that could be said was the faint undertone of live mice. It was a battle she knew not to fight; mice outnumbered Pack by a ratio of seven million to one. In an old house like this, mice were the nature of the beast. The thought made her chortle. Who would know the nature of the beast better than she?

Every other Pack member on the planet, for starters. You have to admit, Rachael-girly-girl, you're a beta. You're the second spear-carrier from the left, the kid in the play who has no lines.

True enough. And irrelevant now.

The kitchen, tucked around a corner to the left, was small, with all the disorder and filth found in the average operating room. In other words: immaculate. Possibly sterile. Back home, Rachael never cooked . . . she had a three-ring binder, organized by cuisine, stuffed with menus from every take-out and delivery joint on the Cape. So the small fridge, half-sized stove, and lack of counter and storage space suited her nicely.

The living room was also festooned with several rugs (mostly reds) as well as a daybed, built-in book shelves (dens for her books!), and a plasma screen television. That made no sense until her landlord, a perfectly nice older gentleman whose name was Call Me Jim, explained that their nephew worked at Best Buy and was always bringing them electric doodads at a severe discount.

"Those plasmatic TVs, they hurt my eyes," he confided while giving her a tour. "But you know kids. If it's new, it's gotta be the best, and if it's the best, you gotta have it. Our old one works just fine."

"That's very generous of you, Mr.—"

"Call Me Jim."

The small bedroom was large enough for a queen-sized bed, an end table with a lamp, a closet, and a small chest of drawers. More than adequate. And the bathroom just off her bedroom had a shower, tub, medicine cabinet, enough rolls of toilet paper to build her own fort, and lots and lots of old towels that were faded but clean and smelled like cotton and Tide.

Best of all were the windows. There were several, and though they were small for house windows, they were large for basement windows. If she stood on her tiptoes in virtually any part of her den, she could see out—a perfect view of the backyard, the side yard, and the side street. And it was much harder for someone to see in.

She had liked the apartment as soon as she'd seen it, and she knew why. It was her den. It wasn't so small she felt claustrophobic, nor so large she felt intimidated by the empty space trying to swallow her. (She had no idea, none, how Michael tolerated living in that enormous mansion by the sea.)

In it, she felt closed in and safe. She supposed it wasn't very interesting as far as individual characteristics went. Pack members liked small spaces they could call their own. She was Pack, ergo she found the basement apartment both comfortable and charming.

Dull, dull, dull.

She went to the rolltop desk and woke her laptop, which kicked right into her e-mail account. Nine new ones. A *thanks for doing this* from Michael. A *come to my next show!* group e-mail by comedic Einstein Jim Gaffigan. A *here are the new movies out this week* from Netflix. And six from Edward, whose e-mail account was (and why was she surprised?) PicardRules666.

"I've assumed by now you were a figment of my imagination.

A smokin' hot spectacular figment. On the off chance I *haven't* gone clinically insane, when can I see you? How's tomorrow? Or tonight? Or an hour from now? Or right this second? Am I coming off as creepy or obsessive? Because I'm neither, I think. Did you know your hair smells like strawberries? Why do I now want a huge bowl of strawberries? It's summer, why can't I find strawberries? Call me, call me, oh for the love of God, please call me: 651-249-3377."

The others were more or less the same. She could feel the silly smile spread across her face and didn't especially care. So she hit reply and typed, "Tonight's good. Come by my new place . . . remember how we agreed our new living situations were sad? Mine's not so bad. Pop by 369 Summit Avenue, any-time after six P.M. Sincerely, Strawberry Fields. P.S. I have no idea if you're clinically insane, and don't much care."

Then she memorized the queen's address and looked up the quickest way to get there. She memorized the directions, made sure her den was secured, and left.

What if you don't make it back in time?

A fine question. Rachael stood on the sherbet porch and pondered.

Am I worried about being killed in her house, or missing my date with Edward? The fact that I have to take a moment and figure that out is sad, sad, sad.

So she mentally shrugged and went on her way.

Twenty-two

Rachael stood on the porch for 607 Summit Avenue. The three-story mansion was white, with black shutters. Relatively fresh paint job; no more than three years old at the most. A front wraparound porch that put her small sherbet porch to instant shame. A detached garage—again, something she was used to, given where she had been raised.

I didn't call for an appointment. I just came. Mrs. Cain knows what I'm doing, but no one else.

Still: I'm here to warn, not engage. We'll see if she has the intelligence to see it. And if she jumps me, or sics underlings on me . . . then I'll know, won't I?

She rang the doorbell. And was surprised: instead of an

old-fashioned chime, the doorbell blatted the chorus from "Cell Block Tango."

What the hell?

Faintly, from what she assumed was the middle of the home, she heard hurrying footsteps. Then the door was yanked open and she was face-to-face with the skinniest African American she had ever seen. With the largest pregnant belly she had also ever seen.

The woman greeted her with a sharp, "Byerly's grocery delivery?"

Hunger. Irritation. Hunger.

"No. My name is—"

"Well, why not? Can't you see I'm starving here?"

Rachael believed her. The woman didn't have an ounce of spare flesh that hadn't been diverted to her gestating belly. Her hair was skinned back so tightly her eyebrows arched in permanent surprise. And Rachael could actually see the woman's blue T-shirt shifting as the gestating spawn moved and kicked.

"I can absolutely see you're starving here. Perhaps you should sit down." She knew nothing about how humans procreated, and this one looked ready to burst into labor on the half second. "Maybe I—"

"Oh, you might as well come in." The woman stretched up to peer over Rachael's shoulder, doubtless seeking the grocery truck. "My name's Jessica." *Hunger. Irritation.*

"I'm Rachael Velvela. I come from my cousin, Michael Wyndham, who is my Pack—"

"Dammit! Delivery the same business day, my black ass." She scanned the street once more, then sighed and stepped back to let Rachael come in. She slammed the door hard enough to muss Rachael's hair. "Heads are gonna roll."

"I believe you." Gestating humans, she had decided, were somewhat terrifying. This small dark-skinned woman looked capable of any violence. And who would dare hit her back, risking injury to the infant? "I'm here to—"

"Well, finally."

Rachael turned to look. A tall, good-looking blonde with shoulder-length hair (and red lowlights) was galloping down the eight-foot-wide sweeping staircase. The front hall was easily as big as the average living room; these living quarters were perfectly suited for royalty. Since she was related to some, she ought to know.

"About time you got here."

"It is? About time?" Rachael asked.

The blonde on the stairs snorted. "Duh, yes. We've had her stuff boxed for weeks."

"Antonia's stuff?" Rachael guessed.

"Duh, yes."

They think I'm here to collect the late Pack member's possessions. Is that good for me, or bad for me?

"You are the vampire queen?"

The blonde, who looked to be in her late twenties, grimaced. "Ugh, yes, and it's Betsy, okay? Do not call me that other thing. Once you pick it up, it's, like, impossible to quit."

"Your Majesty—"

"See? You heard that, right?" Betsy pointed to the one who had spoken, a small woman with long blond curls who didn't look a day over seventeen. She had appeared from nowhere and was hurrying toward the small group. The mansion was doubtless a warren of long hallways and secret entrances and many, many staircases. "She's never gonna get out of the habit. I've been trying for years, and it's still 'Your Majesty' this and 'Your Majesty' that."

Nothing. Nothing. Nothing.

"Your Majesty—"

"See?"

"—forgive my intrusion but I've been going over the monthly—oh. Hello. I thought I heard someone at the door." The teenager squinted at Rachael. "You are not human." *Nothing. Nothing.*

"Not since the operation."

Silence. Stares.

Ouch, tough room. "Uh, no, I'm Pack. I apologize for not calling ahead, but time is not on our side. I was sent here to—"

"She's here to get Antonia's stuff." *Hunger, hunger, hunger!*

Rachael tried again. "Not really, but—"

"Oh! Yes, it's all packed. You must relay our sympathies once again to your king." The teenager looked as distracted as she sounded; clearly she had other things on her mind. "We're running out of freezer space. So I suggest we purchase a chest freezer to be kept off the kitchen in that little nook no one uses."

"We wouldn't need a freezer or a nook to put it in if you didn't buy eighty flavors of vodka." *Nothing. Nothing.*

The teenager blinked slowly at the queen, like an owl. She was wearing khaki knee-length shorts and a red polo shirt; an unbuttoned red cardigan was thrown over her shoulders. Sockless, her tiny feet were pale and perfect. "Yes, well. I do buy eighty flavors of vodka, thus we do need the space." *Nothing.*

Rachael immediately remembered what she, and every other Pack member she'd discussed this with, tried so hard to forget. The most disconcerting thing about vampires wasn't how indestructible they were. And it wasn't that they had their own rules of behavior. It wasn't even that they were technically dead meat walking. No, the scariest, awfulest thing about vampires was only this: they had no scent. No scent.

At least, they had no scent the Pack could detect. Which was unnerving, to say the least. Rachael was used to reading scents almost unconsciously, the way humans read facial expressions. But with vampires, there was no way, no way at all, to guess what they were thinking, or what they would do next.

Unnerving? No. Frightening.

The small pregnant woman was starving and angry—most likely the former because of the demands of pregnancy, and the latter because of hormonal influences.

But the two vampires? Were they angry? Hungry? Bored? Irritated? Sexually aroused? Indifferent? Murderous? Amused?

No way. No way at all to know until they acted.

No wonder you forgot. They're terrifying! That's what they call a psychological block, and small wonder.

"This," Betsy said, once again noticing Rachael, who was frozen in the entry hall with no idea of what to do. "This is what I have to put up with! Dead girls swilling vodka shots. Werewolves dropping by to pick up clothes for other dead girls." She was wearing a dark rose linen shirtdress, belted at the waist, and the prettiest gold strappy sandals Rachael had ever seen. And she, too, was wearing a heavy sweater over everything.

Rachael belatedly realized it was warm . . . almost hot . . . in the mansion. *Of course. Their blood doesn't flow like ours. They're likely cold all the time, poor creatures.*

"You're a werewolf, right?" the queen was asking. She snuggled deeper into her sweater. "That's what *Pack* means, right?"

"Yes, but—"

"There is also the matter of all the fruit we keep frozen," the teenager added sharply, "to satisfy your cravings for smooth—"

"Irrelevant, Tina, you nag from hell!" Again, to Rachael: "See? See?"

"Perhaps," Rachael began, "this is a bad—"

"We'd better not be out of fruit again," the scrawny gestating woman said, growing (Rachael wouldn't have thought it possible) more hungry and alarmed. "Are we fucking out of fruit again? There was a ton of it last night!"

"The driver will be here soon, Jessica, so fret not," the teenager, Tina, soothed. She had a slight southern accent and put across confidence and calm with her voice and gestures. Probably not a teenager, then. She could be a hundred years old for all you know. "Then you may gorge on all the fruit and steaks and Pop-Tarts you like."

"Ohhhh . . . don't talk about the food I can't have right now because the cupboard's bare . . ." Jessica actually clutched her stomach and moaned. "Sooo hungry . . ."

"This is definitely a bad time," Rachael decided aloud.

The blonde snorted again. "Ya think?"

"I shall return."

"Okey-dokey." For an undead monarch, the queen was quite laid back. "Don't let the door slam you upside the head on the way out."

Hostility . . . why? I've done nothing. Or do they resent the reason for my presence? Their perceived reason: that I am here to put their friend to rest, the final act to wipe Antonia off their radars?

Or is it something else?

How will I ever tell?

By coming back, she decided. As often as was necessary. She certainly wasn't going to warn any of them about the murders. Not until she thought about what she had just now seen. Rachael disliked acting on impulse. In this, she was very different from Pack. Before now she hadn't realized it could be a tactical advantage.

"Sorry to have troubled you."

"Are you kidding? This was the least troubling part of my whole day!" The vampire queen laughed, and Rachael found herself warming to the young woman. The laugh, she decided. Fun and carefree. It made her want to—

Rachael got out of there. Fast. Some people, she knew, could make you like them. It was a knack, like being able to raise one eyebrow. She imagined the queen's charisma came in handy more than once. So it was past time to go.

"Next time, maybe you could bring some Pop-Tarts?" Jessica called as Rachael hit the porch.

Next time, I'll bring some howitzers.

Twenty-three

At 5:59 P.M. central standard time, a blue Prius with rental plates pulled into the alley beside the Victorian. Rachael knew this because she had been sitting on the sherbet porch, chatting with her landlords and thinking about vampires.

From the little she'd seen, that was not a mansion filled with terrified minions. Or any minions, possibly. And the queen had seemed more annoyed by their antics than by a werewolf just dropping by. It was perfect camouflage. Or the queen really was that stupid and shortsighted. Not to mention easily distracted.

No, it was an act. Had to be. Because the alternative did not bear pondering. The alternative—

"That last cupcake won't eat itself," one of her landlords

reminded her, so she (ever mindful of being a good houseguest) complied.

She liked Call Me Jim and his wife, Please Call Me Martha. They weren't intrusive but did welcome questions about their own lives. They were both outstanding bakers—apparently they were retired, and their son (Turret Boy, whom she was cordially jealous of because of where he got to sleep) ran their business now.

Retirement did not keep them from baking pies and lemon bars and brownies. It did not prevent them from baking snickerdoodles and peanut butter cookies and coconut macaroons. It was no impediment to the baking of croissants and strudel and sticky buns and apple turnovers. Nothing stopped them from whipping up chocolate donuts and maple Long Johns and fried cinnamon rolls. Certainly nothing got in the way of their creating strawberry tarts and *Svenska* tortes and Boston cream pie (which they had made the day she moved in, in her honor!).

Because they were so busy ripping through pounds of flour every day, Rachael felt it was only the barest politeness to eat whatever they wished to offer her. She was merely being a good guest. A very good ravenous guest with an enormous capacity for pie.

Which is why Call Me Jim and Please Call Me Martha were sitting with her on the porch, watching with satisfaction as she sucked down the last of the devil's food cupcakes they'd brought her.

"Young lady, damned if I know where you put it," Call Me Jim observed. *Amusement. Admiration.*

"I used to be able to put it away like that, but then I had kids. Never have kids, Rachael." *Resigned. Amusement.*

"Mmmph ggmmph unnph," she replied. Umm. Homemade buttercream frosting, surely a gift from the gods.

"You stop that, Martha, you know you wanted kids more'n I did." Call Me Jim was as weathered as a saddlebag but much friendlier and more talkative. He was slouching in his usual outfit of ancient jeans and a faded flannel shirt, long sleeves, black dress socks, and sneakers. Like the vampires, Call Me Jim was always chilly. "There wa'ant no shuttin' you up 'til you caught preggers."

"Says the guy who didn't have seven months of morning sickness, not to mention eighteen hours of drug-free labor." *Irritation. Amusement.*

"Good God, woman, it was thirty years ago! Let it go."

"Twenty-nine and six months."

"Nnnph gmmph," Rachael added, feeling she ought to contribute to the conversation. And that was when Edward roared up. Well. Pulled up, though his little sewing machine car engine made it sound more impressive than it was.

"Hi!" he called, bounding out. *Happiness. Happiness.* He was carrying a large grocery bag stuffed . . . with what, Rachael could not guess. "Am I late?" *Anxiety. Happiness.*

She managed to swallow the last of the buttercream, and gurgled, "Not at all. You're a minute early."

"Traffic," he said, and shrugged.

"These are my landlords. This is—"

"Call me Jim."

"Please call me Martha."

"Hi. Edward Batley." He beamed and wrung their large wrinkled hands. Then winced as the bakers, made tremendously strong from years of slinging dough, wrung his back. "Ah. Ah! Oooh, that smarts. I won't lie. Eesh." He gingerly took his hand back and flexed the fingers.

She grinned to read his shirt: "I Appreciate the Muppets on a Much Deeper Level Than You."

"What the hell is a muppet?" Call Me Jim asked, eyeing Edward's proud logo.

"Oh, you know. That puppet show from the late seventies."

"I didn't watch puppet shows in the late seventies."

"Well, if you did," his wife reminded him helpfully, "you'd know what the boy's shirt meant."

"Hope you weren't waiting long, Rachael."

For twenty-nine minutes, actually. But it wasn't Ed's fault she got tired of waiting inside. *Besides,* she had told herself, *he might get lost. I should be available in case he needs directions. He might drive right past and never realize.*

Sure.

"It was too nice to wait inside," she said, as likely an explanation as any. Too bad it was a lie. "Want to come in?"

"Sure!" He almost tripped coming up the porch steps but caught himself at the last minute. "Ah, man. I hate when that happens."

"Boy's got it bad," Call Me Jim observed, and Rachael couldn't help but laugh when Ed reddened.

He smiled and shrugged. "So? It's the truth."

Charmed, Rachael forgot all about vampires, baked goods, retired bakers, and the murders.

Too bad.

Twenty-four

"It's your very own hobbit hole!" Edward exclaimed, delighted. He had prowled through the small apartment after dumping his grocery bag on the kitchen counter. "It's so cool and cute!"

"Thank you." He was correct. It *was* cool and cute. She was pleased he thought so . . . and wondered why she was pleased. What *was* Edward, exactly? A diversion? A possible boyfriend? Pack members weren't known for dating. They tended to hook up—and stay hooked—early. The drive to create a stable environment for cubs was strong. Always, always they remembered how vastly the humans had them outnumbered. "I liked it the minute I saw it."

"It's got everything . . . you can even see out the windows."

"Yes."

"So." He looked around again, then looked at her. "What d'you want to do? I brought some stuff . . ."

"Oh?" She stalked him toward the kitchen. He was backing up, and she was certain he didn't realize it.

"Yeah . . . I thought . . . a picnic . . . on the bluffs?" *Lust. Anxiety. Happiness.*

She had him backed into the corner between the fridge and the counter. "A picnic?"

"Yeah. I . . . brought some . . . stuff." *Anxiety. Lust.*

"Stuff, hmm?"

"Yeah . . . uh . . . are you all right? You look a little . . ."

Horny?

". . . crazed. Like, with bloodlust. Believe it or not, I actually know exactly what that looks like—yeeek!"

"We should have sex more," she told him, fingers busy with his belt, "and talk less."

"Can't we do both?" he gasped. *Lust. Lust. Lust. (Concern.)*

"I don't know." The belt buckle came free, and she whipped it out of the belt loops. "Can we?"

Lust. Lust. Lust. Lust. Lust. Lust. (Concern.)

(Concern.)

"Wait!" He reached behind them, found the grocery bag, groped, then seized and brought out . . . "Read this."

Annoyed . . . her own lust had climbed quite high by now, something about his scent, that delicious clean-cotton-musky-male scent he had going on worked on her like a hormone shot . . .

but now she forced her hands to be still so she could focus. She had *no* time for, or interest in . . . "This is a lab report."

"Yeah."

"Why have you brought a lab report?"

"Read it," he insisted. "Just read it and—aaaggh! Hands! Hands in naughty places!"

She snatched the paper away, probably faster than he could track. *Calm yourself, you horny tart. Pay attention. The lab report is, God knows why, important to him.*

"This says . . . it says you are disease free."

"Right. Like I told you. Remember?"

Vaguely. Before they'd gotten naked in the hotel room, he'd assured her he was disease free. Which she already knew. He had also apologized for not having condoms. Which she also knew . . . and didn't need. She wasn't in season and so could not get pregnant. And she had no diseases he could catch, and never would. But rather than explain the blood chemistry of the average Pack member, she'd fucked him silly. And had assumed that awkward part of the mating dance as applied to non-Pack members had been permanently set aside.

Not silly to him. He doesn't KNOW you won't give him a disease. And he thinks YOU don't know. So he's brought proof. It's a NICE THING, you horny bitch! Show some gratitude!

"This is a nice thing."

"Uh." He was backed up into the tiny kitchen corner. "What?"

"This." She waved the paper at him. "This is a nice thing. Thank you. For this nice thing you have done."

"Sometimes I get the feeling you're some kind of cyborg."

"Thank you."

"It, um, wasn't a compliment."

"All right. Although this wasn't necessary; I believed you earlier. I knew you were rudely healthy. There was no need to get a lab involved."

He grinned. "Rudely?"

"Oh, yes. I, however, do not have a lab test to show you. I can only ask you to believe that I am disease free, and in fact, before the other night, had not had sex for at least—"

"Don't tell me that again. It's just too depressing. When a hottie of your extreme caliber can't get laid any day of the week she wants, there's something really, really wrong with the world."

"So then." She opened her arms. "Help me make it right."

So he did. Enthusiastically. All over her hobbit hole.

Wait. Did I refer to myself as a hobbit hole, or my apartment as a hobbit hole?

Fuck it.

Twenty-five

"Ummmm . . ."

"Right."

"Ah, God."

"Right."

"I'm numb . . . everywhere."

"I warned you that might happen."

Edward groaned and sat up. "Ow!"

"Careful." She sat up as well and tried to examine his head in the gloom. The sun had been trying to set for the last hour.

"What the hell?"

"You hit your head on the desk."

"What the hell!"

"Sit still; I can't look at it if you keep wriggling." She smelled sweat and semen and musk, but no blood. Felt the top of his head. No swelling. "I think you're all right."

"Tell that to my concussion."

"I was."

They were beneath the small rolltop desk in her living room. She had no idea how they'd ended up there. They had begun in the kitchen and moved to the floor beneath the plasma TV, and for a little while they were in her tub . . . probably . . .

"I'm hungry."

"I'm not surprised. I saw you gobbling down those cupcakes right before you jumped me in the kitchen."

"It's called being a good guest."

"Oh, is that what it's called?"

"Did you bring me food, or just lab results?"

"I brought Oreos," he said. Then, helpfully, "And milk, and a jar of peanut butter and some sandwich bread."

"Nectar of the gods!" she exclaimed, and scrambled from beneath the desk.

A few minutes later, they were lying on her bed, wolfing down peanut butter sandwiches.

"You mean to tell me," he said thickly through peanut butter, "I could have brought this sack for a first date and not dropped a ton of money on fresh seafood?"

"I told you to let me pay."

"Because that's just weird, Rachael. That is *Outer Limits* weird. You are a weird girl. Which is *so* hot, incidentally."

"Thank you." She stared at the Oreo in his hand until he handed it over. "Thank you!"

"I don't think you're even chewing." He was peering at her, grinning. "I think it all just rockets into your gullet."

"Does not. Shut up." She licked her fingers. "Still want to have a picnic on the bluffs?"

"Now?" He glanced out a window. "It's almost dark."

"Yes, I know."

"And you just ate all the food I brought for our picnic."

"Yes, I know."

"We won't be able to see much."

Wrong. I see everything.

"I want to go outside. Can't we go outside now?"

"Sure, Rache. We'll go wherever you want. Don't worry, I packed tons of bug spray."

Which is how they ended up on the bluffs overlooking the St. Croix River at nine thirty P.M. on a perfect August evening, reeking of *N,N*-Diethyl-*meta*-toluamide, also known as OFF! mosquito repellant.

"Oh, my," she said, gazing around her.

"Yeah. I love it up here."

They were seated just at the tree line, overlooking the river. They could see the city of Stillwater below, the restaurants lit up, the streetlights glowing. The river was a black trail beneath them, dotted with little blobs of light from the various boats.

A slight breeze brought dizzying scents to her: grass and

trees and leaves and life. Mating rabbits about thirty-five feet away. White-tail deer cropping grass, sixty feet away.

"You okay?"

"I am very much okay."

"Not too cold?" He'd brought blankets and spread them out with some ceremony. He'd brought more to wrap around her shoulders, though she would never feel the cold as quickly as he did.

"No."

"See okay?"

A bald eagle cruising in the dark. Field mice scurrying for the tree line. A she-possum darting through dense underbrush with young clinging to her back.

"I can see . . ."

A pair of red-shouldered hawks, competing for the same prey, diving toward the cool blue water, only one emerging with a small bass. Their dive startled a heron, and she flapped away. Another bass, much bigger, jumped and arched and fell back into the river with a small splash.

". . . everything."

Oh, everything, she could see everything, and had she ever been so drunk when it *wasn't* a full moon? It was two days away, but in her blood, the moon was full and rising and coloring everything she saw, everything she felt, and had it ever been like this? Ever?

No.

"Feels like we're the only people up here. Not just here. Anywhere."

It did. It did feel like that. Although she felt obliged to warn him . . . "It's an illusion. There's another couple, but they're way down there."

"Really? Gah, I can't see that far." Neither could she. But she could smell them. The breeze was blowing exactly the right way. "You must have kick-ass night vision."

"Yes, that must be it." She reached out, not looking, and found his hand. Clutched it. "Thank you. Thank you for bringing me here. For showing me this place."

"Are you kidding? I'd take you anywhere, Rache. Anywhere you wanted to go. Anytime."

"Then take me now." She touched the back of his neck, pulled him forward, kissed him. She bit his mouth, lightly, and then stroked the bite with her tongue. His lust flared between them, sullen coals one second, a raging forest fire the next. "Here."

"I've mentioned how completely awesome you are in every single way, right?"

"Many times."

"Just making sure. Never let it be said that I take any one thing about you for granted in any way, ever." He was tugging her shirt over her head, yanking at her shorts. She was doing the same to him, while reminding herself not to shred any items of clothing he would need later. "Um . . . we're not gonna have company, are we?"

"They don't know we're here. They're not even looking this way."

"Oh thank God."

"Wait . . . like this."

"Oh my God."

"And like this.

"Oh my God."

"And . . . are you all right?'

"Well, I'm probably going to have a major cardiac event pretty soon. I'm pretty sure my pulse has never been so high for so sustained a period, but I'm okay with it. There are way worse ways to go than dying in your arms."

She giggled as she turned him where she liked, as she went to her knees in front of him, as she put her weight on her elbows. "You won't die, Edward. Probably."

"Oh my God. Your ass . . . it's perfect! You have a perfect ass! How have I not noticed this yet?" She could feel his fingers on her hips, grazing, then grasping. "Oh, who the fuck cares?" Felt his fingers slip between her thighs, find her slippery, dip for a bare moment. "Ummm . . . oh God . . ." Felt him grip her hips, harder, felt that thick part of him start to slide inside.

She met his thrust, hard. His hips rocked back, then forward, hard. She clutched at the blanket, reminded herself not to tear it, and met him thrust for thrust. His groans were dark music to her, the way he sighed and whispered things was a mystic language she had never before known but now spoke fluently.

She didn't know what his favorite color was, or his worst childhood memory, or his allergies (poor creatures . . . *allergies!*), or his favorite dessert. How could she feel so complete with a man she barely knew? Because she felt exactly that, and just as the dictionary defined it: complete. Lacking nothing; whole. Entire.

"Edward."

"Ummm?"

"I'm going to come."

"Oh God."

"Right now."

"Ahhhh! Jesus *Christ*, I can actually feel your muscles—aahhhh!"

Good thing I warned him.

He won't really have a heart attack, will he? She pondered CPR for non-Pack members while at the same time feeling the world tilt as her orgasm bloomed like a black flower.

They met each other for a final thrust, and then he collapsed over her back. "I'm dying," he groaned. "Everything's going dark. Farewell, cruel world, which recently got really awesome."

She giggled. "You can't see a thing; how can anything *go dark*? You're so odd, Edward."

"Me? I'm odd? *Me?* Who cares? Rachael, you can call me anything you like, whenever you like, if we have more bluff sex later."

"Bluff sex." She was now laughing so hard she'd collapsed

forward, losing a bit of breath as the rest of his weight came down on her. "Bluff sex?" She wriggled to poke him in the ribs. "Like all males, now that you've climaxed you are incapable of romance."

"I'm chock-full of romance, you shrew. I'm so full of romance it's leaking everywhere." He poked her back, then grabbed her and gave her a rib-squeezing hug. "This is insane. You're a hologram, I've told you that theory, right? Or I'm pulling a *28 Days Later* and am comatose somewhere while zombies race the streets. Something this awesome simply is not happening in the real world."

"Now: whoever said this was the real world?" If he knew of *her* world, he would believe it.

And for the first time, she started seriously wondering when and how to discuss that world with him. For the first time, that seemed like a natural progression. And as she was an accountant just as much as a Pack member, it seemed quite logical to her. One plus one equaled two. Edward should be told about the Pack so he could make informed decisions. Easy.

Sure.

So they snuggled on their blanket and looked at the stars, thought very different thoughts, and eventually dozed.

Twenty-six

"What the—?"

Edward sat up. He was in his hotel room, in his bed. And he was naked. And he had no idea how he'd gotten there. The last thing he remembered was . . . was . . .

Bluff sex!

Oh my God! Bluff sex!

He booted the covers away and kicked joyously at the ceiling. "Yes, yes, yesyesyes!" It wasn't a dream! Probably! Too bad he couldn't remember anything after bluff sex . . . no. Wait.

There was something else, by God! Yeah, there it was: by the time they'd hiked back to the car, dawn was only a couple of hours away and he was staggering. Not that he was any sort of wimp—he jogged, he lifted, and he occasionally helped Boo hunt vampires. Still: he'd had to give up a lot of, um, bodily fluids recently. Way more than he was used to, that was for damned sure.

He remembered sort of collapsing into the car, then Rachael hauling him out and helping him stretch out in the backseat. Then she'd asked for an address, and he'd mumbled something, and then she'd taken his key card, and then was helping him inside, and then . . .

. . . he woke up.

Had she undressed him? Had he undressed himself in some sort of sexual stupor? Had he never gotten dressed after bluff sex? And why did he care?

I am totally marrying that chick. Assuming she'd even have me.

Right. But first things first: duty called. Only yesterday, when he had no idea things like bluff sex existed, he had met a zombie and figured it was past time to call Boo. But now he was glad he hadn't.

The zombie hadn't hurt him, right? Hadn't hurt anybody as far as Edward could see. In fact, the shambling undead thing had gone out of its way to be polite and helpful. It might be premature to call Boo. He needed to do more recon.

And it had nothing, *at all*, to do with the fact that once Boo flew to town and kicked some collective undead ass, his work here would be done. There'd be nothing to prevent him from going back home.

It had *nothing* to do with that. He just didn't want to waste

Boo's time. He wanted to be sure before he loosed the beast on an unsuspecting undead populace.

It had nothing to do with wanting more bluff sex. And how he couldn't wait to watch Rache put away, oh, half a dozen Subway foot-longs.

It didn't.

It *didn't*.

So: he'd recon. Right now.

Twenty-seven

Though they never knew, Rachael woke up the instant Edward did. The only difference was, she knew exactly where she was, how she'd gotten there, and why she was naked.

"Bluff sex," she mused aloud, and shook her head. And laughed at the sheer silliness of it. The man was good for a laugh, if nothing else. And he was good for plenty else; *nothing* never entered into it.

Her good humor lasted until she picked up her cell and saw a cryptic text from one of two people who had her texting info: "There's been another one."

Cain, with an update. Definitely not Edward.

"Shit," she said, her good mood vanishing. She'd decided against her chat with the vampire queen, and there was a fresh corpse to rebuke her laziness. *Whoever you are, I'm so sorry. If it's any consolation, I won't allow it to happen to anyone else. This I so swear.*

Yeah, sure. If it'd been *her* ghost being appealed to, she wouldn't have been impressed or appeased, either.

Time to see the queen. Right now. Bluff sex would wait. Edward would wait. The lemon icebox pie she knew Call Me Jim was baking upstairs would wait.

She dressed in a blur of motion and ran out to her car in her bare feet. She was so keyed up she never would have noticed, but the vampire queen sure did.

Twenty-eight

She was in enough of a hurry to drive, and parked her car on a slant in the driveway. She hurried up the driveway and, to her relief, didn't even have to ring the doorbell or knock on the door. The dead man had opened it for her.

She slowed. She stared.

The man was not a vampire, and he sure as shit wasn't Pack. He was dead. Newly dead. Newly dead and walking around. But not a vampire. She . . . she didn't understand it.

"I don't understand this."

"Ah, you're back. Tina told me you'd be coming by. I've got Antonia's things right in here, if you'll—"

"Someone is murdering humans to make your friends fight with my family, I think."

The zombie blinked. He was quite handsome for a corpse, with black hair and eyes the color of wet leaves. He was wearing surgical scrubs, which added just the right surreal note to their odd meeting.

"Oh. Well. In that case"—holding the door wide for her—"you'd better come in and talk to Betsy and Sinclair."

And in she went.

Twenty-nine

Horror-struck, Edward was frozen to the spot. He felt like he was in a nightmare. He prayed he was in a nightmare. It wasn't real, right? None of this was real. He hadn't seen . . . any of it. He hadn't seen it. It didn't happen.

It *was* happening. Right now.

Rachael had driven right up to the mansion, exactly like she knew where it was.

She'd parked the car in the driveway at a hurried slant, not caring if someone was blocked . . . she'd been there before and wasn't worried about pissing someone off with a crappy parking job.

She'd gone right into the mansion. *Right* in. Someone had been watching for her and held the door for her. *Held the fuck-*

ing door for her! It was that last that seemed to shriek the implication at him.

He plunged his hands in his hair and clutched hard enough to make his eyes water. "What . . . the . . . fuck?"

Thirty

The polite and helpful zombie led her straight back to what Rachael saw was the kitchen, one the size of a small football stadium. The queen, her assistant/friend/minion Tina, and the starving pregnant angry Jessica were all seated on stools around a butcher-block table.

The air reeked of fruit, and there were many, many glasses on the table, all with varying amounts and types of smoothies in them. There were three, count 'em, three empty blenders plugged in and clearly ready for more business.

"You again," the queen greeted her. "Just in time for happy hour." *Nothing. Nothing.* "Whoa! No shoes, no service, missy! What's with the bare feet? Are you from Arkansas?"

"No." She realized in her rush to leave she'd neglected footwear. What an odd thing for the queen of the vampires to notice. "Forgive me, but . . ." Why was this only now occurring to her? Was she in *that* deep a fog of lust? ". . . why are you awake when it's daytime?"

The leggy blonde yawned. She was either unphased by Rachael's reappearance or possessed a superhuman ability to appear so. "Queen of the vamp perks."

"But she"—pointing to Tina—"isn't the queen." Unless she was . . . what? A co-ruler?

"No, but she's decrepit," Jessica answered, unmindful of her smoothie moustache. *Hunger. Amusement.* "Ancient, even. I guess the older you are, the more godless hideous abilities you get."

"What an apt description, Jessica, thank you so much." *Nothing. Nothing.*

So. The vamp who looked like a walking ad for jailbait (who wore pleated plaid skirts with crisp white blouses anymore, unless they were on their way to a costume party or a fetish convention?) was an ancient vampire.

Good to know. She hoped they would make more slips. If they were slips. Could they be that confident? That unworried?

"I guess that makes sense," she admitted, feeling a comment was required. They were awfully free with their information. Assuming any of it was the truth. She couldn't *tell*, that was the maddening part. Only with the pregnant woman, and who knew what havoc pregnant hormones were wreaking on her senses? "I apologize for coming by, again, without calling first, again, but I need to tell you—"

"Why have you and your friend been sneaking around the neighborhood?" Tina asked.

Rachael thought about that one for a few seconds. The queen apparently saw this as a lull in the conversation, which she jumped to fill: "See? Toldya that'd knock her for a loop. Oooh, gimmee more of that sweet blackberry goodness. Nom, nom, nom!"

"Ugh, how can you stand all the seeds?" The zombie was peering at the queen's glass with poorly concealed distaste.

"*All* fruit has seeds," the queen protested. "You're sitting there with a glass of strawberry *seeds*, moron!"

"There's seeds and there's seeds," Jessica piped up. "You'd never grind up apple seeds in a blender for a smoothie."

"You can't," the zombie said. "They're poisonous."

"They are not. That's an urban legend."

"They absolutely are. Trust me, I'm a doctor. A dead doctor."

"*What friend?*" Rachael asked, much more sharply than she intended.

"Oh, like you don't know. Puh-leeze, think we were born yesterday? It's just not true." The queen nodded toward the jailbait poster child. "Tina, in fact, was born about a thousand yesterdays ago."

"How amusing, my queen."

The zombie cleared his throat. "Betsy, I think you need to

listen to her. She says she thinks people are being killed to get your attention."

"No shit? Well, that's just great." The queen shook her head, suddenly dispirited. "Just when I was thinking my only problem was figuring out how to bring you back to life."

"Don't you dare bring me back to life," the zombie replied sharply. "Then that damned prophecy will come true and I'll eventually become the Marc Thing. Don't make my suicide seem like a mistake."

"Your suicide *was* a mistake," the queen informed him.

"Dammit, Betsy!"

"Dammit, Marc! Like I'm gonna let you shamble around as a fucking *zombie* for the next thousand years? Have you met me *ever*? Not gonna happen! Get it through your thick, zombie head!"

"Excuse me. What friend?"

"Oh, don't worry. My husband's taking care of him right now."

Rachael turned to run, her mind empty of everything but the urgent need to get to Edward *now*, which is when someone turned all the lights out in her skull.

Definitely should have seen this coming, she thought, watching with detachment as the floor rushed up to smack her in the face.

Thirty-one

Edward had no idea how it had happened, but one moment he was skulking just outside the alley, freaking out—

What the hell is Rachael doing there?

—and the moment after that he was dangling in the air from the fists of a shockingly strong man.

"I have not yet decided how dangerous you are. Shall we discuss it, you and I?"

Finally! Someone who dressed and spoke appropriately for a paranormal moment. From what he could see (though things were already going fuzzy around the edges) the guy was huge, tall, broad-shouldered, and dressed in black.

"Outstanding! We gonna talk about it while I die from— gggkkkk!—oxygen deprivation? Or no, wait! Kkkkkk! You can throw me off the roof. Could you say *you shall rue the day you crossed my path* in your deep scary voice while you throw me off a roof?"

"But for my love," Dark Dude muttered, "I would tolerate none of this." He dropped him, and Edward flopped to the ground, coughing and gazing up at Dark Dude.

"You got it right," he said happily. "You got it all right. I'm . . . I'm just so happy. I've been waiting my whole life for someone like you."

"Alas, I am happily, deliriously, eternally married," he said dryly. "And I must say, don't think I've ever seen that reaction before. Why are you here?"

"I'm spying for my best friend, a vampire slayer," he replied promptly. He never hesitated to tell a vampire the truth, with Boo and Greg's fervid encouragement. It had saved his life more than once. The vamp would often get so rattled he or she forgot all about Edward in their haste to get the hell out of Dodge. "And you guys are gonna get it! Zombies and evil baby farms. Be ashamed!"

"I have not the vaguest idea what you are talking about. And I suspect I do not want to."

"She put you up to this, right?" It was starting to make sense. Horrible, horrible sense. *Well, you knew all along Rachael was too good to be true. And now you know why.* "I should have seen it. I really should have."

"You sound a bit like Cape Cod."

"I don't have a Cape accent," he retorted.

"You do, actually, a slight one. That means you're from the coast . . . and that means you are acquainted with Ghost."

Duh. Of course this guy knew who Boo was. Her fearsome reputation had obviously spread to the Midwest. Well, it saved time. He wouldn't have to tell Dark Dude who she was and why he should be deeply terrified.

"Yeah, that's right, pal. And when she gets here, and sees that you've mangled me even a little bit, she'll take it out on your undead ass."

"Excellent."

"What?"

"You must call her straightaway."

"What?"

Dark Dude made an impatient gesture. "I have been aware of her for some time. And I believe she is aware of the recent regime change."

"Totally aware," he lied, having no idea what Dark Dude was talking about.

"Yes. So. Please call her at once and ask her to visit."

"Dude. If I call Ghost for a visit, the death count will hit two figures, guaranteed."

"Do it. As soon as you can. And make sure she has our address."

"*Our* address?"

"It's in the newsletter," he said impatiently.

"Yeah, about the newsletter . . . don't you think it's big-time dumb to—"

"I don't like this. Not any of it. Run along and call for help, little man. I must see to the queen's safety."

"Oh . . . her? She doesn't need protecting. She's in a class by herself." The lying faithless bitch.

"How wise of you to know it."

"Uh . . . how are you walking around in daylight?"

"Call it a perk of royalty."

"I call it freaky and big-time strange. Aren't you going to, I dunno, try to bite me, or threaten me with hideous mutilation, or something?"

"Make sure Ghost has the address. You might want to give her directions, just in case. Or you could just drive her straight over."

"Sure," he said, beyond mystified. "I'll get right on that."

"Excellent. Oh, and young man? If I catch you skulking near my love even once more, I will pull your spine out through your mouth."

Now that was more like it! "Do your worst, you foul night-stalking ghoul of the . . . where'd you go?"

The guy had done a total Batman . . . left while Edward was still getting his bearings.

If not for the awful thing he'd found out, it would have been the most exciting encounter of his life. Well. After bluff sex.

Thirty-two

He'd had his cell on him, of course, and as he walked back to his car, he pulled it out, preparing to do as he was bid, when it rang in his hand.

Boo!

"Hello? Boo?"

"I apologize for intruding, but I must hear about your date. How did it go?"

Not Boo. He sighed and replied, "My Yoda socks were a huge hit."

He could practically hear Gregory's groan of horror all the way from the coast. "I specifically told you *not* to wear them."

"Shows what you know, because she went wild with lust at

the very sight of them. I don't want to talk about her. Can I talk to Boo?"

"You had a nice time with the young lady?"

"Sure." Gigantic understatement. *It was great, until I found out she was the vampire queen.* "And I've never, ever seen anyone (ever!) suck down so much raw seafood in my life. She's from Mass; she loves the fresh stuff. Listen, I gotta talk to Boo, okay? Right now."

"Alas, we are still basking in the afterglow of—"

"Greg. Right now, I'm not kidding. *Put her. On. The phone.*"

He could almost feel Gregory's perplexity and sympathized. *He's never heard my no-bullshit tone of voice before. Probably surprised because I sounded so cool and steely. Like Darth Vader, except without the respirator. No, like Lee Majors! The Six Million Dollar Man!*

Luckily, Gregory did as he was commanded, saving Edward from more steely talk, and then he heard Boo's familiar, "What's up, moron? We were about to head out. What's wrong, you forget to pack your Wonder Woman Underoos?"

"I kept telling you, those weren't mine. I was holding them for a friend."

"Ha! Trapped in another lie. I didn't believe it then, and I sure as shit don't believe it now. You can't expect me—"

"Boo, shut the fuck up."

She was so surprised, she did. *Thank God she's fifteen hun-*

dred miles away . . . like I need a broken nose on top of everything else.

"It's bad, Boo, I'm pretty sure."

"Tell me," she said at once, all traces of teasing gone.

"They've got a zombie."

"I thought you said *they've got a zombie.*"

"I absolutely said *they've got a zombie.* I met him, face-to-face. And I must say, for a zombie, he looks pretty good." Shit, the zombie was better looking than he was, with those green eyes and the black hair. And the scrubs . . . Women probably went nuts for his zombie MD ass. "But that's not even the bad part."

"Great. Hit me."

"I've seen it—him? Not sure how I should refer to him-or-it. Anyway, I've seen him-or-it hanging around the mansion . . . you know, vamp HQ? With the vampire queen? And I've also seen him with a pregnant woman."

"I didn't even know there *were* zombies," Boo admitted. "And I've been killing the undead for over a decade."

"Neither did I, as of twelve hours ago. But it wasn't as alarming as it could have been. Let's face it, when you hear the word *zombie*, you kind of expect the worst."

"No, Eddie," Boo said, kindly enough. "When *you* hear the word *zombie*, you expect the worst. When Greg or I or a normal person hears the word *zombie*, we assume it's because George Romero is still cranking out the franchise."

"Yeah, yeah." Edward was privately impressed Boo even knew who George Romero was. *Years of living with the Geek King actually made an impression on her! Who'da thunk it?* "This one wasn't gross or anything. He didn't try to eat my brain."

"He knew your feeble brain wouldn't even rate as an appetizer. What are you thinking?"

"I don't know. I'm worried—I'm not sure—"

"Come on, Ed. I know you have a series of increasingly outlandish theories, but in the interests of time, and my patience, just run through the highlights, okay?"

"Okay. I'm worried they're sacrificing babies. Why else would a zombie hang with a pregnant woman in a mansion ruled by a vampire queen? I'm scared that the vampire queen is running this whole evil baby ring. I can't prove a fucking thing, though."

"You don't have to," she said at once. "This isn't one of Gregory's *SVU* reruns."

In the background, Edward heard Gregory's sharp retort: "Say nothing against *SVU* or Mariska Hargitay, woman, if you ever want to have sex with me again."

"Blow me, fangirl. Listen, Ed, your theory's good enough for me. If you're right, I gotta get going. And if you're wrong, I'm out a few hours of travel time, so what's the harm? Okay, I'll be obligated to give you tons of unrelenting shit for years and years to come if this turns out to be a false alarm or a fever dream or whatever, and I'll definitely beat you up a little, but better that than overlooking some sort of . . . of . . ."

"Vamp-run evil baby zombie ring," Edward supplied.

"Just hearing you say that makes me tired." She sighed. "But tough shit, right? If I didn't want the job, I probably should have gotten around to quitting."

Edward wasn't sure if vampire slayers *could* quit—what would Boo do if not that? Take up knitting? Learn to bake? But he held his tongue.

"I'll leave tonight if I can get a flight," she finished. "Otherwise, first flight out tomorrow that's got a seat. Okay?"

"Thanks, Boo." His relief was a sweet wave drowning his feeble brain. "I'll text you the addy for my hotel. Come straight here and I'll show you where she lives."

"Done. And Edward?"

"Yeah?"

"Stay away. No more spying. Stay the hell away from now on, got it? This is no time to act like a big-boobed horror-movie heroine."

"Don't worry."

"I'm coming." And she clicked off.

Boo was abrupt, and tactless. She didn't suffer fools (or telemarketers) gladly, and she could mess up a pin-neat living room faster than a toddler hopped up on Mountain Dew. She occasionally talked with her mouth full and heaped scorn upon all things *Star Wars*. She didn't own a single T-shirt with a quirky saying and avoided the Internet when at all possible. Her hideous soulless habits knew no bounds.

And when a friend needed help, she dropped everything and came on the run. Her love and concern and loyalty also knew no bounds. He had always understood why Gregory had fallen in love with a vampire slayer. He was only surprised it had taken him more than twenty-four hours.

Feeling a little better, he got busy with the texting. And then he got busy with the disobeying.

Like he was going to let his best friend walk into a nest of vipers without every scrap of intel he could dig up? He was more likely to corner William Shatner and rhapsodize how Kirk was superior to Picard in every way.

In other words: never, ever, ever, ever happen.

Thirty-three

"Ow." Rachael started to sit up, then clutched the back of her head. "Ow!"

"Wow."

"What?"

"That was scary. One second you were out, and the next you were sitting up. There's, like, no fuzzy period for you guys, is there? You're either dead to the world or ready to fight."

"I've always been a light sleeper," she muttered. "Ow!"

Cool hands on her, pressing her back. "You'd better lie still. Tina cracked you a pretty good one."

"Remove your hand, zombie. Or I will."

"Right. Got it." He removed his hand. "But if you pass out, don't come crying to me."

"Don't worry." They'd stretched her out on a couch in a parlor somewhere. The peach floral print couch smelled like ancient fabric and mouse poop and dust. She sneezed three times. "What happ—never mind. I have to go." She sneezed again. Wretched teeny turds!

"Not just yet, if you please." A new voice. Deep and measured. Thoughtful?

She looked.

It was the vampire king, what was his . . . ? Sinclair. That was it. She'd only gotten a glimpse of the two of them when they'd been on the Cape, months ago, but she would never forget either of their faces.

Especially his. He had the face of a teenager, with stress lines bracketing his eyes and mouth . . . a very old teenager, to be sure! And dressed head to toe in black. In the dark, no one would see him. In the dark, she imagined he did exactly as he pleased.

"Stay a while," he said, pretending it was a request.

Not just in the dark, she realized. *He does exactly as he pleases wherever he is. He's like Michael! He doesn't* have *power, he is* power!

"Why?"

"So we can discuss your future."

"What did you do to Edward?"

The vampire didn't feint or affect to not know what she was talking about. She liked that. "I asked him to call a vampire slayer and invite her to visit."

"That's all?" She couldn't smell Edward on him. But then, she couldn't smell anything on these people. "You didn't hurt him?"

"Don't worry."

"I never *worry*. But if you touched him, you should start. Immediately."

"Yes, yes, right after you remove Marc's zombie hands you'll doubtless introduce a wooden stake to my nether regions, oh dear, oh dear, we tremble and obey."

She could feel her face getting red, and she stood. The zombie flinched back, and she was glad. *Too quick for humans to track, at least, even if the vampire doesn't seem to mind. Arrogant condescending prick.* "I'm leaving. Don't bother seeing me out."

"Oh, come on. Don't go yet. He's a huge pain in the ass, it's true, but he sort of grows on you after a while. Like athlete's foot." The queen's voice, from the doorway. "Look, I found you some shoes. Won't you at least try them on before you do the storm-out?"

Shoes? What? Why the hell should she . . . ? Who *were* these people? She looked around the parlor, realizing that the carpet and wallpaper were also peach.

"I know," the queen said, following her gaze, "isn't it awful? Half of this place needs major updating, but somehow we never get around to it. But hang out a minute, okay? Sink Lair will dial back the jerkiness, I promise."

"Yes, Her Majesty promises," Sink Lair replied helpfully.

"Ah-ha! Thought so!" The queen had crossed the room and held one of the shoes—a pair of navy blue flats in a sort of lacy pattern . . . What did they call that? Peau de soie? Anyway, they were blue flats. And the queen was holding one of them beside Rachael's left foot. "See? Perfect match."

"How did you know they would fit?"

The queen looked guilty. "I, uh, measured your feet while you were out cold."

This . . . is the most surreal thing that has ever happened to me. And I once worked in my uncle's antique shop for a month. During tourist season.

Bemused, she let the queen slip the shoes on her feet, like an undead Macy's saleswoman. "There!"

"Thank you."

"I apologize for mocking you earlier," the king said in clear response to the queen's sizzling glare. "It was not . . . kind. Will you tell us why you came in the first place? Marc said something about murders."

"Yeah, but if I'd known Tina was gonna clip her with the handle of one of the butcher knives, I might have held back."

Clearly ruffled, Tina shot back, "Well, I couldn't just let her walk out."

"Yes!" The queen threw her arms in the air. "You could have! This is why we never have people over anymore, Tina!"

"Softly, my love," the king said, looking at the queen with poorly restrained affection. It was as tender a moment as she could have hoped to see among the undead, and it gave her the strength to tell them what was on her mind.

"Somebody's murdering humans. And the timing is odd. Michael Wyndham sent me out here to keep an eye on all of you—"

"All of us?" Tina asked sharply.

"The king and queen. And no sooner am I here than the body count starts. People who were supposed to be my new clients. I'm wondering if someone is doing it to cause trouble for the vampires and the Pack. Or maybe . . ."

"To cause trouble between the vampires and your Pack," Sinclair mused. "Yes. I see it. Hmmm."

"That's why I came to warn you. It's not me doing it. And if you're not doing it . . . well. As I said. Odd timing."

"It's not us," the zombie said. He glanced around the room. "Right? Guys?"

"Of course not." But Tina said it with such flat affect, Rachael couldn't tell if the woman was lying, or teasing, or neither.

The king had taken a seat beside his queen and was leaning forward, his hands on his knees. It was startling, the way he could go so still. When he moved, it was like seeing a statue move . . . unsettling and odd. Even a little frightening. "Can you get us information on the victims? Police reports, autopsies, anything?"

"Probably." She'd have to find out. Did Cain have any Pack

contacts with local law enforcement? Could Michael make a phone call? "I'll have to make a few calls."

"Do that, if you please. And then come back."

"Of course." *Yes, I'll rush right back into this rat's nest, to be sure. And you might find it'll be much harder to take me from behind next time.* She was furious with herself for that. She might not be able to smell them, but she could hear them. She should have been three steps ahead, instead of getting sapped like a cub. Her concern for Edward had completely screwed up her—

Edward!

"I have to go." She stood. The flats fit perfectly. For some reason, that pleased her, though the idea of a vampire queen measuring her feet while she was unconscious was creepy. "Right now."

"Wait," Tina said. "What is your name?"

"Oh." Hadn't she told them? *Very* distracted in her worry for Edward. "I'm Rachael Velvela. CPA," she added helpfully.

Tina's brows rose. "You're an accountant?"

"Yes."

"A werewolf and an accountant?"

"I have to make a living, don't I? That is, since my kind stopped stealing babies by moonlight."

"Ooooh, ouch, guess we had that one coming. Velvela?"

Tina was frowning. "Isn't that Yiddish for wolf?"

"Yes."

"You're a Jewish werewolf accountant?"

"*Yes.*" What, exactly, was the problem here? "And I must go. Thank you for . . ." Coldcocking her? Mocking her? Giving her shoes? "I have to go."

"Are you okay to drive?" the helpful zombie asked. "Maybe one of us should give you a ride."

"If you're the bad guys," she told them, heading for the door, "you're the most polite ones I've ever seen."

The king grinned, showing a great many white, sharp teeth. "We try, dear. Run along now. Make your calls. Then return."

She sketched a mock salute. *I hear and obey, O Vampire King, except when I don't. You'd better sleep with one eye open. I won't be so easy next time. Nor so pleasant.*

"Hey, those shoes are a loan, you know. Not a gift." As Rachael left the room, the last thing she heard was the queen's wail: "Get anything on them and you'll wish you'd never come to our house and interrupted Smoothie Time!"

Too late.

Thirty-four

Edward looked at his phone, which had started buzzing again. Rachael. The vampire queen. Calling him again. Probably wondering what new webs to spin around him.

It was the next afternoon, and he was in a new hotel. He'd spent most of yesterday checking out and moving his stuff to a place Rachael had never seen. He hadn't been smart enough to figure out what she was up to, but at least he was smart enough to erase his tracks.

He'd been on a geek high after meeting Dark Dude, a high that lasted all the way back to his hotel room. Then it was displaced by reality. He hated when that happened.

When he finally had a chance to sit down and think about the depths of her trickery and betrayal, he wanted to die. He wanted to slap the shit out of the vampire queen. He wanted to set her hobbit hole on fire. But mostly . . . yeah. Die. Or if not that, at least never to have met her. Never known the joys of bluff sex.

Your own fault. You knew. Knew she was too good to be true. Maybe the newsletters were a trap, ever think of that? And she caught you.

Sulking on his bed, he flung his forearm over his face and groaned as the full horrific realization nailed him yet again between the eyes: that awesome girl, that super-sexy Rachael Velvela, was the soulless degenerate depraved vampire queen.

Ohhhh, it all made sense. Her façade as a friendly gorgeous chick who did *not* gulp the blood of innocents was perfect. Their fake run-in at the bookstore . . . She obviously had spies everywhere. It was all part of her plan to get to Boo. And he'd fallen for it, hadn't he?

He'd lived with a vampire and a vampire slayer for years; he couldn't believe he hadn't spotted her for what she was. Oh, the betrayal, the deceit! A flawless performance, especially when she would . . . would . . .

"Bluff sex." He sighed. "Oh, fuck me."

Well, she wouldn't have him to kick around much longer. He'd seen to *that*, if nothing else.

Except . . .

His eyes widened as a new-yet-horrifying thought rocketed into his mind: Boo was coming. Except he hadn't really put together what that meant. What it meant for *Rachael*. He hadn't seen the logical conclusion of his phone call.

The vampire slayer *was coming*. He'd called her himself. And when Boo showed, Rachael was dead.

How had he not thought of this before? He wasn't just betrayed, wasn't just a sucker for a gorgeous face . . . it was a lot worse. Half his damned brain seemed to have shut down!

And here was more proof, though he sure didn't need it: if he was running with all faculties at systems go, why was the thought of Boo carving the queen a new mouth so upsetting?

Yeah, why? Huh? How many has she killed? Look what she's been up to in the short time you've been here. Look at what she was planning! Evil zombie babies! Hurricane Boo was on the way; the smart choice was to hammer the windows shut and hunker down until it passed.

Yep. That's what he would do. He would hunker until it passed.

Absolutely.

Yes.

His phone buzzed again. He grabbed it, then answered with a curt, "Your place. Twenty minutes." He didn't wait for a reply.

He lunged for his car keys and left the room so quickly he didn't even lock it.

Thirty-five

She answered the door at once, pale and nibbling on her lower lip. "This isn't a good time."

"Tell me about it." He stomped past her and down the stairs to her hobbit hole. "Let's go, toots."

"Toots? Really? And why haven't you been answering my calls? Dammit, Edward, I've been worried about you!"

"Big fucking deal." He stopped in her living room, turned. Faced her. "I know, Rachael."

"What?"

"Quit it. I know."

"I do not have time for this, Edward." She snuck a glance out one of the windows. "Very soon I'm going to have a . . . a biological dilemma. You can't be here when that happens."

"What, like your time of the month?" Suuuure. Vampires didn't menstruate. He was pretty sure. How dumb did she think he was?

Pretty dumb.

"Exactly. My time of the month." For some reason, she laughed. "Except not what you think. Edward—"

He grabbed her. "Rachael, listen to me. *Listen.*"

"Why," she asked mildly, "are all your fingers digging into the meat of my arms?"

"I know, okay? I *know.* And my friend Boo is coming to kill you. You have to get away; I have to get you away. She. Will. Kill. You."

"What's a boo?" She was prying off his fingers one by one, still much more interested in the view than anything else. "Something dreadful, probably; you smell like cotton on fire."

He felt like shaking her. He let go before he did. He was so afraid he would hit her. So afraid.

Curse those vampiric senses! "Never mind how I smell. You gotta leave. Like, right now. *Right* now."

"I can't go anywhere *right* now. In fact, *you* should leave. I shouldn't have let you come over at all. I had . . ." Another peek out the window. "I had other things to worry about, but I was also worried about you, and tomorrow morning we're going to have a big wicked fight about it, but you have to go now."

"Will you cut the shit? Huh? I'm telling you, we have to go. So will you pack already?"

"No. You get out of here."

"I know you're the fucking vampire queen, Rachael! And the greatest vampire slayer in the history of vampire slayers is probably on a flight to here right now!"

He was expecting a heated denial, or cold mockery. Anything but what actually happened: she laughed so hard she fell down. Actually fell down! And laid on the carpet holding her stomach and laughing up at him.

"Okay." He stared down at her. "This isn't going the way I planned. At all."

"Me! The vampire queen! Oh . . . oh . . . oh!" She snorted and giggled. "Oh, that's rich! That's wonderful! Me! One of them!" Then she sobered. "Wait. How do you even know there's such a thing as a vampire queen?"

"Why d'you think?" he snapped. "I got your stupid newsletter. It's got your damned address in it."

She blinked up at him. "Who *are* you?" she asked after a long moment. "Who are you really? You're not one of them. And you're not one of us. So who are you, Edward?"

"A fucking moron who believed you actually—" No. He wouldn't tell her that. He wasn't even sure why he was trying to save her. Only that he had to. *Had* to.

"Look, enough with the slinging of crap, okay? Even if you won't admit it—"

"I will not admit it." She shook her head. "Ever."

"I can prove you're her." He bent and seized her wrist and

pulled. She rose like smoke to her feet, so easily it was like she had no weight at all. Then he started to tug her toward the door but couldn't move her any farther.

Puzzled, he thought, *She must have set her feet against something.* He tugged harder. *Something like a cement bookshelf? Maybe the rolltop desk was heavier than it looked. Except she's not touching the desk.* He was so intent on exposing her web of lies that he didn't ponder. "I can prove—unf!—you're the vampire queen. Save yourself some trouble and—nnnf!—admit your evil plan to—nnf!—enslave babies. Or make babies into zombies. Or zombies into babies."

"I admit nothing. Certainly nothing about zombie babies. You can prove this?"

"Yes."

"Well." He had tugged again and nearly fell into the doorway. Suddenly Rachael was halfway to the door with him. "Prove it."

He hauled her out of the hobbit hole, past the porch, and into the yard, and they both blinked in the late afternoon sun.

"See? See?" He pointed at her, and had never felt triumph warring with despair so strongly. Ever. "You're *not* a pillar of screaming, shrieking flames. See?"

"Your proof is that I'm *not* on fire?" The lines he loved (when he thought she was the coolest girl ever, as opposed to what she was) appeared on her cute, wide Christina Ricci–esque forehead. "I think you've been reading the wrong books about vampires, because in actuality, they are incredibly vulnerable to—"

"Just stop it. Okay? Cut the shit." It was the sunshine, so bright, bouncing off the chrome and steel of their rental cars. It was his sweat glands getting their signals crossed. He was so angry his eyes were leaking. It was one of those things, because he *was not* crying. Not over the fucking vampire queen.

"It's not just that," he continued. He was tired. So tired. "You always seem to know exactly how I feel. When my mouth says one thing and my brain another, you always know what I'm talking about. *Always.* Roommates I've lived with for years don't know what I'm talking about. The day we met I thought about how intuitive you were . . . but it's not intuition. It's just more vampire bullshit. But no more."

"Edward."

"God, I had the clues right in my fucking face all week and couldn't see. Your body is perfect, there's not a mark on you. Of course you don't have a mark on you! You're dead, you heal from everything. Everything!" He smacked himself in the forehead, hard. "How stupid could I be? Jesus!"

"*Edward.*"

He slashed his hand at her. "It's over, Rachael. And you will be, too, if you stay. So you gotta go. Now."

For a wonder, she touched his face. It took everything . . . *everything* in him to jerk back from her small, delicate fingers. "Edward, Edward. I've deceived you, yes, something one accountant and Picard lover should never do to another. But I'm not doing something strange and evil with babies . . . or zombies . . ."

"Rachael, will you please cut the shit?"

"Well, I'm not. And later, I'm going to ask you why you thought that. And I'm not even a garden-variety vampire, never mind their ruling sovereign." She laughed again. "I'm a nobody, really. I'm the kid in the play who has no lines."

This time, he was the one to laugh. "That might have worked a couple of days ago, Rache. Not anymore, though. I *saw* you. Don't you get it?"

"Edward, you must . . ." She trailed off when he twisted away from her outstretched hand, and hurt flashed into her expression like a cramp. Now he was the one who wanted to reach out. Which just proved what a fucking fool he was, and had been, all this time.

"Go. You have to go. Just . . . get out of this city, this state. Don't ever come back. She'll kill you if she can find you. Don't get found. Don't, Rachael."

"I'm not a vampire, Edward." She smiled a little and glanced to her left. Nothing over there except another meticulously maintained mansion. And the summer moon, which looked like an enormous silver disc, almost looming over them. "And *I* can prove *that*."

Thirty-six

"Once upon a time, about a zillion years ago, there was a great ape and a dire wolf. Or a *hominid* and a *canis*."

"Rachael . . ."

"Shut up!" she screeched. "Shut up, it's my turn, you had your turn and now it's mine so you be quiet and let me talk now!"

Edward flinched back. He looked awful, pale and drawn; his face looked as bad as hers probably did. For certain, he was as stressed. Her teeth had been on edge the moment she'd opened the door. But she had never considered leaving the door closed, never considered ignoring him until she was ready for him.

And why would she? It wasn't his fault. None of it. But that didn't change the fact that it was her, har-de-har-har, time of the month. Not just that but her time in a strange city with no friends, no friendly faces. She knew she would have to endure her Change alone, and just that fact made it something to dread.

How stupid we all are, she thought. Many a month on the Cape she had made plans to stay in and spend her Change quietly on a rug in front of the fireplace, and it had been nothing to her. Now that she *had* to stay in, *had* to hide, suddenly it was a hindrance, a burden, a *cage*.

Thus she was a teensy bit on edge. PMS? Sure . . . times a bajillion. She didn't worry she'd pick a fight with Edward. She was worried she'd pull his nose off his face and stuff it down his throat.

"So." She tried to force calm as she formed another hamburger patty. They were sitting at the picnic table in the backyard. Her landlords, thankfully, were out—they and the son were attending a family reunion in Mahtomedi, wherever the hell that was. They were out until the wee hours, maybe even overnight, and by then things would be . . . would be settled. Yes. By then Edward would be made to understand, and he'd also be gone.

You can't keep him, she reminded herself, nibbling on the hamburger. *You mustn't try. Tell him and show him and then stay out of his way. It will be all right. His opinion is nothing to you. A week ago, you didn't even know his face, never mind his scent. A stranger's opinion is nothing to you.*

The backyard was small, and fenced, and overlooked a

clothesline and a fire pit that hadn't been used in at least ten years. The small yard and accompanying view were sort of dreary, but it was outside. Soon enough she'd have to closet herself into the hobbit hole for the night, so she would take what night air she could, while she could, and she wouldn't be a picky snot about the view, either.

And while she did, she would snack and tell stories. Edward probably liked stories. And if he didn't, or wasn't in the mood because of his absurd theory, *who the fuck cared, and if he had half a brain, he wouldn't come up with stupid ideas about vampires, forcing her to change her plans for the evening at the last second when it really wasn't a good time goddammit!*

Whoa.

She took a breath. And another. And another. *Stop panting.* "And there was nothing special about that ape or that dire wolf, except the ape lived in Africa, and the dire wolf was native to North America. And over the course of many, many years, the ape evolved into a man who used tools, and the dire wolf evolved into a woman who hunted in packs. And the man was human, and the woman was Pack. I'm Pack."

"Uh-huh." Edward was sitting across from her at the picnic table, watching her. She knew he—

anger anger anger lust anger confusion sad anger anger

—was still upset. But not afraid. At least he wasn't afraid of her. *God, never let him be afraid of me, oh please, never that.*

"Great story, Rache."

"It's not a *story*," she snapped, momentarily forgetting that she had told it to him exactly like a story. "Okay, it was. It is, but it's also relevant to now. I'm not a vampire, Edward. I'm Pack. A werewolf."

"Uh-huh."

"Say something besides *uh-huh!*"

"Okay. How much more of that raw hamburger are you going to eat?"

"What?" She looked down. The burger she'd formed into a patty, then nibbled, was the fourth in three minutes. Her bag o' meat was now empty. "Oh. I'm . . . I guess you could say I'm a stress eater."

For the first time that afternoon, he smiled. "Then you're stressed every minute of every day. Look, I get that you didn't want me to figure out your secret. And I don't know why you set out to meet me at all, except maybe it's got something to do with Boo. It's the only thing I can figure. But it doesn't matter now. I don't think I can call Boo off, she's sort of like a button you can't un-push, so you've got to—"

"I don't care."

"What?"

"I don't care that you can't call Boo off. Let her come." She licked her fingers. "She can't hurt me. She'll see I'm not a vampire, and even if she doesn't, she won't be able to hurt me. Then she'll probably lay into you for a while for sending her on a wild vampire chase, which I'm going to find hilarious. And then she'll go away. Leaving me to figure out who's killing every-body."

"*What?*"

"Which part of that freaked you out?"

"All of it! Jesus! Okay, first off, you don't know what the hell you're talking about."

"That's true, but only for one of us."

He ignored her, too busy waving his arms around and rant-ing. "Because second off, Boo can *absolutely* hurt you, all right? Boo can hurt the bejeezus out of you! Third off, she's not going to 'go away' until she . . . and who's killing everybody? I think you skipped a step. Who's a killer?"

"I don't know. That's what I have to find out. The vampires might help." She thought about it. "Might. Her if it doesn't interrupt Smoothie Time, and him if he thinks it might be a danger to her, or them. I haven't decided if they'll be a hindrance or not. I don't have that data. You definitely will be, running around telling Pack members they're vampires . . . that's just not helpful, Edward. It's not. You're staring at me again."

He was. "And there's a good reason for that! I can't believe we're having this . . . okay. Look, I'm not mad—"

anger anger anger concern anger fear anger

"—anymore. I mean, I am, but, but we've got to talk about this. We've got to figure it out. At the very least, you're delu-sional. At best, Boo's on her way to kill you a lot. Either way, you're in trouble."

Either way, I'm blessed. You are a darling, Edward, a darling pain in my ass. What a fool this Boo must be to have let you leave her!

"Have you ever known a vampire to eat full meals? To eat solid foods of any type?" she asked, waving the now-empty Ziploc gallon bag at him. She'd been tempted to turn it inside out and lick it clean but reminded herself Edward had been through enough already. No need to put him through *that. Just one of those nasty things we only do when we're alone.* "Ever? Hmmm?"

"You're the queen vampire," he said stubbornly. "You can do stuff the others can't. We went through all this. That un-vampire-y stuff, it goes with the territory."

"Not at all. I'm Pack. I'm sent by *my* leader to watch *their* queen. And I don't know why you're here at all . . . except it's not just to enjoy a change of scenery, is it? Edward? I was sent, and I never thought to question why you were. Did your Boo send you?"

He was shaking his head. "She's not *my* anything, and no. I sent myself. Should have done it sooner, frankly, because I had to get the hell—we're not talking about me, dammit! We're talking about you."

She peeked at the moon. Soon. Soon. It was almost time to go inside for the night. Because she had to, she didn't want to. She could be so stupid sometimes, so contrary to herself. *Because I have to, I don't wanna. Wanna stay out here with Edward and feel his anger and lick empty Ziploc bags. Waaaah!* Pathetic.

"—why you picked me, but it's not like we didn't have some fun. I don't want to have to tell you these things, Rache, but I don't want to keep them corked inside me, either. I don't want to think about how even that kiss in the bookstore was a lie, just like—"

C-R-A-C-K!

"That kiss was not a lie!"

She didn't understand the noise right away. Then she felt the spreading numbness in her hands and realized she'd brought her fists down on the tabletop, hard enough to smash a crack right through it. And Edward had listened to his inner ape, quite sensibly, and was now on his feet.

The look on his face. It was almost funny. It wasn't just what she'd done to the table. She knew what it was; she could feel the tension in her jaw. She hadn't shouted, exactly. She'd sort of . . . sort of *squeezed* the words out through her clenched teeth. It was closer to a growl than a shout.

"I—I don't know how to lie in a kiss," she said, and burst into tears.

Thirty-seven

She wasn't sure when or how, but Edward was sitting beside
her, which was a sizeable improvement over standing apart from
her and saying cold things and hating her, wanting to hurt her.

"Oh, Rache, please don't . . . don't . . . don't," he pleaded,
giving her halfhearted pats on the shoulder. "You're upset . . .
okay. Your cover's been blown, or whatever. But no harm done,
okay? There's still time to get out of town. Just don't—don't do
that, okay? I really can't stand it when you—oh, Rache. C'mere."

Then . . . miracle! He was hugging her and patting her and
whispering to her and her head was on his shoulder and he—

concern concern concern lust anger concern concern

—wasn't hating her anymore. He was being nice again. He
was being wonderful again.

"Just . . . calm down. Let me see your hands, you almost broke the table, you probably have splinters down to the second knuckle . . . there! You're okay. Huh. There's not a mark on—right, we covered that. We know how you can do that. And it's okay!" he added hastily, as if worried she'd burst into fresh sobs. "Well, it's not *okay*, but you know what I mean. Look, let's talk about—let's—okay. Say I believe you. Tell me how it happened."

"How what happened?" she sniffed, surreptitiously wiping her nose on his shoulder.

"Well, I did see you over there, in your—in her driveway. We both know you were there. Tell me about it."

"About what? You said you saw me."

"Sure. What were you doing? If you're not the vampire queen, why were you there? How'd you even know to go there? Let's say I'm buying this bullshit you're tossing . . ."

She straightened up, freshly pissed. "Bullshit I'm toss—?"

He put his hands up like a man being arrested. He'd turned, they had both turned so they were straddling the picnic bench, their faces only a foot apart. "So you were . . . what? Sent on a noble and sacred mission to spy out the land?"

"No, apparently, *you* were. Which reminds me! I've got a few questions for *you*, pal."

"Focus, Rache."

"*You* focus." She sulked on her part of the bench, but he was apparently done with the comforting. Now he was like a bloodhound on the scent.

"How did you creep into town all unnoticed by the vampire queen's sinister minions? Assuming you're not her?"

"I didn't creep."

"What are you, a lawyer or a slammin' hot accountant?"

"Oh, I never could have handled law school," she said, appalled. She shook her head. "Too many gray areas. Accounting, at least, is black and white. One of the few jobs that *is*, really. Nothing like social work, or medicine."

Edward sighed and ripped his fingers through his hair so fast she was worried he might accidentally scalp himself. Or give himself a friction burn. He took a deep breath—

Forced calm. Anxiety. Irritation.

—and started again.

"Okay, Rachael. From the beginning. You skulked into town . . ."

"I *drove* my *rental car* to the chamber of *commerce*, where I met with a . . ." *Pack member*, she'd been about to say, but her secrets were her own to share. She had no business outing any other Pack members to Edward without their permission. ". . . a woman who had sort of prepared the way for me. She'd set up my living arrangements and was trying to get some clients for me. I didn't know if I'd be here for a week or a year or a decade, so I needed to try to build a bigger client base."

He nodded, reached up, and tucked a stray strand of hair behind her ear. "Okay . . ."

She loved that he did that. She loved that he didn't know he did that.

"And then, once I knew where I was going to be living, I got settled in—didn't take long, I can tell you." She sort of gestured to the basement. "You've seen it."

"Yup. And . . . ?"

"And I made note of the address from the newsletter. I kept it."

"Which you had because . . ."

"My cousin is our Pack leader. He's the boss werewolf. He had one and he made me a copy."

"Unreal," Edward muttered, passing his hand over his eyes as if getting a headache. "Vampires are either fearless or stupid or maybe both."

"I," she retorted, "am not arguing. So I had the newsletter, I had her address. I MapQuested it, walked there since my apartment is only two blocks away from her mansion—far enough away so I'm not in their line of sight, but close enough so I can get there in a hurry if I have to. Or leave in a hurry if I have to. It's a huge neighborhood. It's not hard to lose someone if you have to."

"Logical," Edward said, nodding. Then he jabbed a finger in her direction. "But still sinister."

Rachael sighed and peeked at the moon again. She didn't have to, not really. She could have been in an underground bunker (which maybe the hobbit hole was, come to think of it) and would have known exactly what phase the moon was in at all times. Still, she had to look. The moon was her jailor and her lover.

"Then I rang the doorbell and was courteously let inside."

"You didn't call."

"No."

"They had no idea you were coming."

"No."

"Fearless or stupid."

"Yes, or something beyond that, something we can't understand. Perhaps it's because they live so much longer than we do. Their slow—nonexistent, even?—metabolism spreads a different message. They have perspective we don't have. Or can't understand."

"Yeah, maybe. That's . . ." He trailed off, thought about it. "That's interesting. Huh. So they let you in."

"Yes. Because, see, I didn't know it at the time, but they thought I was there to collect . . . This is going to sound complicated, but another Pack member used to live with them. They thought I'd come for her things. They weren't surprised to see me. And they weren't afraid, either. When I realized that, I decided to come back another time. I wanted to think about what I'd seen. I wanted to ponder what they'd done, and what they hadn't done. So I left."

"You saw the queen, though?"

"And her assistant, and a pregnant woman. And a . . ." She paused. Thought about it. Went ahead anyway. "I don't expect you to believe me, because you haven't believed anything I've said today, but I also saw a for-real *zombie!*"

"I know, right?" he cried, his hands on her shoulders, almost shaking her in his excitement. "Really good-looking guy, green eyes and scrubs? Right?"

"Amazing!"

"I knoooow!" He realized they were nose to nose and pulled back. "Okay. So we can agree that whole zombie thing was cool and weird."

"Very cool," she agreed. "And very weird. I didn't even know there were zombies."

"Jeez." He was watching her in that strange way again, as though he couldn't make up his mind if she was a freak or a find, or both. "If you're lying, you're the best I've ever seen."

"I'm not lying." She tossed her head. "But I *am* the best you've ever seen."

He laughed, surprising them both. Then sobered almost at once. She was sorry. But at least he was—

concern concern puzzlement concern perplexity

—listening. At least he was trying to keep an open mind, even if he truly didn't know what to think.

"You said your Pack leader, you said he sent you out here. To Minnesota. Why?"

"We're cousins. He trusts me and he knew I'd do what he

asked for love, not duty. He knew I wouldn't want to go, but he also knew I wouldn't let that get in the way of the work."

"Yeah? So you guys are close?"

"Yes," she said simply. There were too many things to explain in the course of one evening, especially *that* evening, and Pack dynamics were one of them.

"Are you gonna get in trouble for telling me all your secrets?"

"I'm not," she replied, amused. "There isn't time to tell you all my secrets. But if there was, the answer would be no. He loves me and he trusts my judgment."

"I can see why he loves you." Edward nodded. "Who wouldn't?"

Oh, Edward. Do you even know what you just admitted to me? And the answer is, lots of people. Lots of people wouldn't. Daresay couldn't? But I love that you can't understand that.

"But," he continued, "why send anybody?"

"Because the last werewolf he sent to keep an eye on the vampire queen turned up dead in less than two years.

"What?"

Thirty-eight

She nodded. "It's true."

"Jesus!" *Worry. Worry. Fear. Fear. Worry.* "They killed her?"

"No. She took a bullet for the queen."

"She did what?"

"I know. She died. We're a hardy bunch, Edward, and we can take a lot of punishment compared to your kind, but even we can't grow our own frontal lobes back."

For a moment she thought he was going to fall off the bench. His look of shock and horror did more than touch her heart; it gave it a cramp. *Oh, Edward. You're too good.*

"And he asked you anyway?"

"Yes."

"And you went?"

"Of course."

"Because you're his cousin and he knew you'd go."

"Yes!" she said, pleased he was catching on.

"Then he's a prick and I'm going to beat the shit out of him!" the accountant roared. "I am not believing this shit even as I'm hearing it! He's a dead man, Rache! That shit! That fucker!"

"But that's so sweet! Truly, Edward. I love that you said that. But you mustn't be mad at him."

"Yeah? Mustn't I? Just watch."

"My duty became my pleasure about five seconds after I met you. If I'd known you were waiting, I would have come here much sooner.

"Ah, Edward. Stop me if you've heard this . . ."

" 'I'm not the vampire queen'?" he guessed.

"Well, yes. But also, you're too good. Anyone else would have greeted me with a stake through my upper ribs."

"Yeah, well. It's not even the weekend yet. So then what? We'll get back to your asshole cousin. What happened after you met them?"

"When we finished 'visiting,' I let myself out. I wasn't so much gathering info as I was indulging in a quick gossip with the gals (and zombie). Which is when you spotted me."

"No, because I didn't see you then. I saw you the next day. Right?"

"Ah! Yes. Because after bluff sex, my contact in downtown St. Paul texted me about another murder. I realized that my wanting to see you had actually cost some poor creature her life. When I realized the depth of my carelessness, I went back to the mansion straightaway."

"Me, too, me, too!" he interrupted excitedly. "I'd blown off calling Boo because I didn't have the smoking gun. Any gun. So I wanted to see what else I could find out. That's when I spotted you." This time he was the one to sigh. It sounded like a soft breeze through a cemetery.

"That's when I knew it was all over but the cleanup. You . . . and me . . ." She opened her mouth to interrupt, but he shook his head. "I might have given her the wrong information on purpose. I mean, to delay her. Which I'll pay and pay and pay and pay for. But we've got a little time now. I figured I'd let Boo come and just get out of the way and let her do what she does. You know, like Hoover brand vacuum. But I couldn't . . ." He was looking into her eyes as his own shone with tears that hadn't dropped. "I couldn't just . . ."

"Throw me to the wolves?" she guessed. "So to speak?"

"And here we are."

Her heart didn't break, nothing that dramatic, but it did get a tiny cramp when she took in Edward's crestfallen expression.

He really wanted to believe in a world right out of a Xanth novel and, of course, wanted the truth here and there, but could never hide how bummed he was to discover yet another thing he relied upon was about as interesting and romantic and magical as track lighting.

The latest reality check? The mystery gal is just another spy spotted in the wrong place. It's nothing. No, it's even worse than nothing . . . it's explainable.

Edward's problem isn't that magic isn't magical, she thought with deep sympathy. *His problem is, he's the biggest romantic I've ever met. He wants knights to slay dragons and then marry the Maiden Fair and live happily ever after. He wants all that, he would live for all that. He doesn't want to back up servers and coordinate audits.*

But no matter what it is, what paranormal stereotype he encounters, it's always both more than it seems, and less.

"This time I was able to warn them—the vampires—and they warned me. They knew you were out there."

"Aw, man." He shook his head with a rueful half smile. "And here I thought I'd been so sly."

"Nope. Don't feel bad; you weren't bred for that sort of thing. That's when I—" She paused. Took another look at his expression. "Well, they told me that one of them was taking care of you. I was—I didn't know what that meant. I was afraid I did know. So I . . ."

"Rode to my rescue?" Edward clasped his hands to his chest and sighed as he fluttered his eyelashes. Typical of men who don't give a shit about such things, he had long, lush eyelashes, the lucky bastard. "Did you, Rache? Ride to my rescue on your . . . uh . . . steed?"

"Turned my back on one of them long enough for her to clip me with a sturdy knife handle," she said dryly.

"*Her* being the vampire queen?"

"Oh, no. No, it was her friend, the beautiful little blond girl who dresses like she's late for Catholic school."

"Um . . . okay. We're gonna circle back to that, because I didn't get to meet that one, wouldn't you know it."

"I can't see the queen throwing a knife at anyone," she admitted. "A bottle of nail polish, maybe."

"But one of them did."

"Yes. My own stupid fault for turning my back on people I knew to be predators. I deserved worse for forgetting such a fundamental rule of survival." She shook her head, disgusted. "Must be old age setting in."

"Ha! What are you, twenty-four, twenty-five?"

"You're adorable. Thirty." Of course, the jailbait vampire could have a hundred years on her for all Rachael knew. "It was humbling beyond belief."

"One of them . . . just so I'm following the sequence of events, here . . . one of them threw a knife. At your head."

"Well, yes. But it's not as bad as it sounds."

"Rachael!"

"It's not," she insisted. "For one thing, she could have flipped the blade. Having the pointy end zip through the back of my skull would have put a sizeable damper on my day."

Edward was pressing his hands to his face. "I'm pretty sure you're giving me a migraine. I'm . . . I've got to tell you . . . aw, man, I'm having a freak-out aneurysm here! I can't decide which thing to yell at you about first."

"There is kind of a long list," she admitted. "I'm sorry for adding to it."

"So what happened next?"

"I woke up in an orange parlor."

"What?"

"No. Stop. Let me think." She closed her eyes, saw the room in her mind, smelled the mouse poop in her mind. "Peach. It was a peach parlor. The sofa and the walls and even the carpet. It was like waking up inside a womb."

"Okay, that's so weird I'm actually trying not to picture it."

"And the vampire queen had measured my feet while I was unconscious and gave me a pair of blue flats to wear home."

"She did not!"

"You're right, now that I recall . . . she loaned me the shoes. She didn't give them."

"Rachael! Of all the weird, idiotic, and/or scary things you've told me, that's the least believable. And think about the list of things you've told me!"

"You're right, you're right . . . it's a terrible long list. No wonder you're getting a migraine." She stole another glance at the moon. She was closer, now. Well, of course she wasn't, not really; it was an optical illusion. But it was a beautiful, sweet illusion and one she cherished. The moon looked closer because her Change was closer. It would come closer still, and then Rachael would be the moon, be in her. And then for three nights she would be herself, her true self.

"Oh, ya think? Listen . . . no, wait. Are you okay? You've got a really strange look on your face."

I'll bet I do. She almost laughed. "I'm fine, relatively speaking."

"Okay, good. But like I was saying, I haven't actually met the woman, which you're gonna rectify for me just as soon as—"

"I certainly will not," she said sharply. "You're to stay away from them, Edward. We've both been careless enough."

"Yeah, hold your breath and see if that'll happen. But listen, I don't know her, but I do know this: the queen of the vampires doesn't just hang out in her big spooky mansion to drink smoothies with zombies who are taking care of the pregnant woman who also hangs out there (I assume for prenatal smoothies). And she sure as shit doesn't give visiting werewolves pairs of shoes!"

"Lend," she corrected. "She lent me a pair of shoes."

"Whatever! Vampire queens don't do that stuff. No self-respecting monarch of the undead would do any of that stuff."

"Up until seventy hours ago, I would have agreed. Now I can't. I think that's the trick."

"What?"

"I think that's why her reign is working. She doesn't do anything the way you'd expect. It's a pretty good trick." More: she suspected that was Michael's underlying motive in sending her here. Not just to keep an eye on things. To figure out why things were working the way they now were. Infinitely more valuable information to have. "It's a trick I'll bet my cousin would like to learn. But that's a talk for another day. We've been out here as long as I dare." She stood, peeked at the moon, held out her hand. "We have to go inside now. I have to, I mean."

"So you can change into a werewolf."

"Yes." *Change into* always made her smile. Like it was something the Pack could take on and off, like a dress shirt. It would never occur to her to ask Edward to *change into* someone with white skin and blue eyes.

"Yeah, well, I believe you when you say you're not the vampire queen—I'm pretty sure—but I gotta call bullshit on this werewolf thing. Not that I think you're lying," he added when she opened her mouth. "I think you could take a polygraph and never bounce a needle. But that proves my point about you needing help. You can't ask me to believe that every full moon . . . Let's just say I'll believe that when I see it."

Thirty-nine

"Aaaaaaaaaaaaaaagggggggggggggggggggghhhhhhhhhhhhhhhh!"

Forty

Edward had tripped over the rolltop desk and hit the floor hard enough to actually see stars. *Wow,* he thought, rubbing the back of his head. *Look at that! Actual stars. All those Bugs Bunny cartoons were telling the truth.*

It was his fatal mistake, of course, and his death was coming in the exact manner he had always known it would: he'd gotten killed doing something idiotic or clumsy or both. So he wasn't at all surprised when the slavering she-beast of the night rushed over to him, jaws dripping foam, snarling her hatred for man, her ancient enemy.

Except what really happened is that she let out a surprised yelp—

(funny, weird and funny that it seemed more like a gasp of dismay than a yelp, funny how it was like she wasn't all person and she wasn't all wolf, funny how it was like she was something in between a creature that was both and neither, all the time, yes, very funny)

—and rushed over to him, anxiously sniffed him, then tried to lick the back of his head.

"Wh—aagghh—stop it, that tickles!" What he had first mistaken for slavering jaws dripping enraged foam was the friendly wide wolf grin (accompanied by a lashing tail) he'd seen on canines before.

"Oh boy," he said, bringing his hands up again to push her away, and letting them drop to his sides again. "Ohhhhh, boy. If you don't devour me in a bloodlust born of a dire feeding frenzy, Rachael, I owe you a gigantic apology. Like, the Galactus of apologies."

She was still trying to get at the back of his head. "No, it's fine, Rachael. Just a bump. You—you—" *Scared the shit out of me! Made me watch my life flash before my eyes, and y'know what? It wasn't that great a life!* "You startled me."

And it was his own damned fault. *She warned you. She wasn't cute or coy about it; she flat-out told you; I am a werewolf and I am going into my hobbit hole to change into the form of a wolf by the light of the full moon, so smoke 'em if you got 'em.*

Or words to that effect. But did he believe her? Noooooo. And why should he? It wasn't like he had, oh, I dunno . . .

firsthand experience in tons of weird paranormal shit due to the fact that he LIVED WITH an ex-cop/current-comedian vampire and an albino vampire slayer!

Perish the fucking thought.

No sooner were they in her apartment than she began stripping off her clothes. This had the (perhaps predictable) effect of every coherent thought fleeing his mind as blood raced from his brain into his dick. "Uh, Rache, not that I don't love seeing you naked, not that I don't love just the very thought of bluff sex—or would it be hobbit hole sex? Anyway, I think if we have sex now, it would fall under the taking-advantage-of-Rachael category."

"Please stop talking."

"And not that—whoa, bra shooting past my shoulder! You ever notice that those can be used as slingshots? Wow, you're really whipping them off, aren't you?"

"You're still talking." Her voice had gotten lower; she sounded pissed, so he figured shutting up wouldn't be the worst idea he'd had, and then she, and then she, and then she—

(Say it!)

—and then she turned into a wolf.

If he'd blinked, he would have missed it: one minute she was naked and hairless and cute and pale and pink, and the next she'd dropped to all fours and was hairy and grew a tail from somewhere and her ears got longer and her snout got longer and her teeth got much, much, much—

(Why grandma!)

—much, much, much bigger and longer and sharper, and then he was shrieking, not so much from fear, okay from a little fear, but also shock and surprise and the sheer joy of it; he was screaming with the knowledge that Rachael was beautiful in every mood, in every form Rachael was—

(my God, Rachael, you're so beautiful I didn't know anyone could be so beautiful)

—beautiful.

Cue Edward staggering backward; cue Edward tripping over desk and hitting his big stupid skull.

And now, he was locked inside the den with the she-beast! She'd led him back here in her treacherous human form, she had led him into a basement that didn't have an exit for a wolf, she'd penned him up with her, and now he was trapped in the lair of the beast!

The beast had taken a moment before devouring him to rush over and make sure he was okay. Oh, the deceitful cunning of this ravenous monster knew no bounds!

Dude: lock it down, will ya? You're embarrassing yourself.

Good advice. "Quit it, Rache, I'm fine." Again he brought up his hands, but this time found the courage to very, very, very gently rest tented fingers on her shoulder as he gave her a very, very, very slight push.

Well, she didn't bite any of his fingers off. That was something. Emboldened, he increased the pressure. She didn't budge, nor did she devour.

"Don't worry about me, it's my own stupid fault and it's just a bump. But you can't stay in here all night. Can you?" He'd never imagined such a thing. Maybe real-world werewolves didn't howl and hunt. Or at least, howl and hunt during the entirety of the full moon. Maybe some of them stayed indoors.

"Shouldn't you be roaming the countryside looking for chickens? Ow!" He glared at her and rubbed the spot on his shoulder where she'd nipped him. "Okay, sorry about the stereotype. Not very PC of me. Listen—no, I'm fine." He gave her another shove. It was like trying to knock over a fire hydrant. Then she gave him another nip, her teeth and jaws so quick he felt the mild pinch before he realized she'd moved at all.

"Okay, o-*kay*! Jesus. You're a nag in every form, anybody ever tell you that? Look." He dropped his head and she sniffed the part in his hair. "Don't worry, I cleansed myself thoroughly with Suave Mountain Strawberry. You may sniff me without fear!" She already was, so he figured he might as well give her permission.

"Okay, I know what you're thinking. But it isn't like that! Okay, it's a little like that." He absently rested his hand on her lush dark fur. "Listen, this is gonna sound pretty dumb, but when I was in your bathroom the other day, I saw what you used for shampoo, so I went out and bought some for my bathroom so it would be like you were there. I know, I know. Just so lame, right?"

That was when he realized what he was doing. He was speaking to her like she was a real person. Like she could understand him, like this was a *conversation*. How cool was that?

Then he slapped his forehead, hard. *Of course she's a real person, you nimrod! What, you were expecting a hologram? Didja think she was a computer program?*

He examined the almost-invisible nip she'd given him with her teeth, Rachael-ese for, *Do you think you can stop acting like a dumbass for ten whole seconds?*

"Y'know, that's twice you've subjected me to your unholy jaws. What if I turn into a werewolf during the next full moon? Hey, is that it? That's it, isn't it?" He sat bolt upright with excitement. "That's why you picked me! You want a boyfriend who you can run with by the light of the full moon, a mate who shares your passion for the hunt as well as a Quicken spreadsheet. It all makes sense now!"

She laughed at him.

Okay, it wasn't exactly a laugh. Her canine grin widened and her expression got downright playful . . . amused, even, and he . . . he could just tell. She was laughing.

"Fine, I guess I deserved that."

Her eyes were exactly the same.

He looked closer. Yes, it was true. She was a little different on the outside, but her eyes, those gorgeous tip-tilted pools of deep brown, and what was behind her eyes, was the same.

In that moment, he knew that for the rest of his life he would always be able to spot a member of Rachael's family, her Pack.

It was nothing he could have taught someone. It was nothing he could have described. Recognizing Pack was like riding a bicycle: it couldn't be taught, you had to learn it yourself . . . and once learned, you could never un-learn it.

Her fur was also deep brown, lush and thick as the hair on her head when she walked on two legs. He gently flattened his hands on her pelt, then smoothed it, then stroked it. It was like stroking a combination of velvet and wool. Wolf fur, he realized, was like the taste of chicken: hard to describe, but unmistakably its own thing. It wasn't velvet and it wasn't wool; it was wolf fur; it was Pack.

Bolder, he ran his hands all over her, curious and fascinated and awed all at once. Her ears were scuffed velvet and pricked forward alertly. Her long sleek snout was much darker than the rest of her, and—

"Wow. Just how many teeth do you have, Rache? I would not want to meet you in a dark alley. Okay, I absolutely would want to, but I wouldn't want to meet another Pack member in that alley. Though I bet you could take 'em.

"And speaking of taking 'em, how lucky was that vampire dumb enough to throw a knife at you? You could have bitten her whole face right off! I mean, you could have run home and waited a couple hours for the moon to rise and then changed into a wolf and then run back and bitten her face off. And serve her right," he added, enraged all over again at the thought of someone throwing a lethal weapon at Rachael's head.

Though he admitted to some bias: he wouldn't have liked it if someone had thrown a nonlethal object at her, either. Like a packet of shoelaces, or a baby's pacifier. Oh, the humanity! Wait. Did that even apply here, when one of them wasn't human?

"You just wait. Once you get me back over there, that vampire's gonna apolo—ow! No. *No*," he added firmly, rubbing his now-stinging elbow. "I'm not bending on this one, Rache. You can nibble on me until I'm skeletonized, you're still taking me over there and introducing me to those knife-wielding psychopaths.

"I mean, how could they? You came in peace, right? *Me* acting like an asshole is one thing; I've acted like a true dumb shit this whole time. It's not a new thing to the world. But they're supposed to know better. They're . . . they're the grownups! And me, I was just . . ."

He shook his head and ran his hands over her fur again. Then he buried his face against her side. "You're so beautiful, Rachael. How could I not have seen it? How could I have been such a hateful dumbass?" He thought of the things he'd said earlier and went cold. "Mine was the face to bite off, if anybody deserved having their face bitten off. If you forgave me, it'd be a miracle."

He sighed into her fur, which smelled like soap and green grass and werewolf, Rachael's own special smell. "If you forgave me, I'd spend the rest of my life trying to make it right. If you forgave me, I'd never take your good faith for granted. If you could just give me that one chance, Rachael, a chance I've done nothing to deserve." He swallowed a sob and rubbed his eyes, hard. On top of everything else, he wouldn't subject Rachael to his ongoing immaturity, his babyish lack of control. He didn't want forgiveness as a result of her pity and his shame. *Lock it back, dumbass.* "I'm so sorry. I'm so sorry."

She only looked at him, then leaned forward and snuffled behind his ear, the exact spot she'd pressed many kisses in the last week. Then she yawned, circled once, and curled up beside him.

And then she went to sleep.

After a few minutes, he said, "It's wrong to find this anticlimactic, right? Grateful is the emotion I should be going for, right?"

Then he leaned back against the wall and dozed off, his hand resting on her back.

Forty-one

Rachael opened her eyes, surprised to find herself a) in her bed, and b) alone. Now last night of all nights, where would Edward—

She heard the door open, heard his light, eager step stop outside her bedroom door. He poked his head in and brightened when he saw her. "You're awake! And you're the other you again! Awesome."

She was startled and touched by *other you*. Many people would have said *back to normal*, and she would not have taken offense. She loved that Edward had so easily grasped that she wasn't part human and part wolf; she was all Pack. It was a tricky concept for non-Pack to grasp, and the centuries of negative press from fairy tales didn't help.

"Oh my God," he said, looking horror-struck. "You're *awake*. Oh, Rachael, I'm so sor—"

"Shut up now, will you?" she said kindly. From the look of him, Edward had been up most of the night with her. He had that starry-eyed need-a-nap-but-too-keyed-up-to-sleep expression. He had seemed to spend the night waiting for her to do something. All night he'd waited, and there had been no way (beyond the obvious) to tell him that curling up in a hobbit hole listening to crickets and the evening breeze *was* the plan. She believed he'd finally caught on around four o'clock in the morning. "You had cause."

"I didn't, Rache. You're nice to say so, but I absolutely didn't." Forgetting he had an armful of grocery bags, he rushed to her side of the bed. *Regret. Regret. Sorrow. Shame.* "I was *such* an asshole."

"I know you're sorry, Edward. No need to keep on about it."

"Mmmm . . . nope." He appeared to do some sort of inner analyzing. "Nope. I'm still crushed with remorse and feel the need to keep cowering and groveling. Not that you didn't leave tons of clues, because you did, but you even *told* me (more than once!) and I still took that as my cue to try for Douche Bag of the Year."

She started laughing at his given title, but he didn't so much as smile. "For a guy who considered himself open to paranormal shenanigans of any kind, I turned out to be stupidly close-minded."

"*And* a contender for Douche Bag of the Year," she teased.

His face, pale with tension, suddenly lit, and this time he was laughing with her. "Have you considered where you're going to display the trophy?"

"I should probably have a case made, huh? Listen, I just got back from Cub Foods . . ." She rose from the bed and padded after him to the kitchen. "You were all out of raw hamburger and milk and Pop-Tarts."

"I loathe—"

"Yeah, well, they're for me, so just back off. Also, it's un-American not to like Pop-Tarts."

"Why do I hate America?" she mused aloud. "Because I sure do. America and everything she stands for, including Pop-Tarts. Hatred fills me at the mere thought of a chocolate fudge Pop-Tart."

"Yeah, well, that's what I'd expect from a Cape Cod liberal pinko werewolf."

"Hey!"

"You heard me," he said smugly.

"I'm no pinko, you ape-evolved troglodyte."

"Hurtful." He sighed, putting on an expression so pious and sugar-sweet she wondered if he'd have an insulin reaction. "So, so hurtful." He brightened. "And here! See? I got the seventy-thirty hamburger mix. By the way, the explanation for your unstoppable appetite for everything in the *world* finally occurred to me about four A.M. And again, let me say to myself: duh."

"And eggs and juice and pork chops," she said approvingly.

"I didn't know . . . I thought maybe you'd be pretty hungry once the sun came up."

She smiled at his anxious expression. "Don't worry, I hardly ever eat people anymore."

"Ho-ho-ho. But seriously: please don't eat people. I figured you'd be hungry."

"Nope. That Ziploc o' Meat bag is still holding me. But this was thoughtful . . . I keep telling you, you shouldn't pay for me to eat. Ever. You realize if you keep it up, you'll eventually have to take out a loan."

"I know, now." He laughed, then tentatively reached for her. "Did anyone ever tell you, you're gorgeous on all fours?"

"Well, of course *you'd* think so," she teased, delighted to see him blush. She hadn't thought he'd flee. Hadn't *thought*. But there was no way to ever truly know about someone until they were facing what you feared.

"That, yeah, ask me if I think bluff sex could cure all the world's problems—but I meant—I meant your other self. Those four legs."

"People have told me that, yes." She reached up to push his bangs to the side, out of his eyes. "But only other Pack members. You're the first—I mean, you're my first—" Now it was her turn to blush. *Fair's fair*, she thought ruefully. "I've never slept with anyone who wasn't Pack."

"Ah, but you know the old saying. Once you go off Pack,

you can't wait to head back. No. Wait. That's not it." He pulled her into his arms and nuzzled her neck. "Once you renounce the Pack, you have to try out for track? Now that you've been exposed to Pack, you're gonna have to hire yourself a hack? Closer, I think . . ."

She reached down, past the waistband of his shorts, and found him already thickening. "The next time we need a motto, I promise you'll be the first one we call." She squeezed gently and heard his soft groan. "The very, very first." *Lust. Lust. Lust.* "Have I mentioned . . ."

"Yeah?"

"I love your scent."

"Ummmm . . ."

"I absolutely love it." Squeeze. Release. Squeeze. He was unzipping his fly to give her more room, but she ignored it. Squeeze. Release. "You know the only thing I like better than how you smell?"

His groan was drawn out and his eyes were rolling up; he tried to speak and could not.

"How you taste."

Forty-two

"What now?"

Rachael stretched beside him. They'd made it back to her bedroom . . . eventually. "Food?"

"I was thinking about the long term."

"More food?"

He jabbed her in the ribs and she shrieked and jabbed back. "Agh! Yes, yes, we'll stop by a slaughterhouse on the way to the bluffs and you can gorge until you blow up."

"Ooooh. Too mean."

"For reals?" His smile had faded at once as he watched her face.

"No, but . . . borderline. More a girl thing—does this wolf

form make my butt look big?—than a Pack thing, though, in your defense."

"Got it. No more slaughterhouse jokes. Are there any racial slurs I need to be aware of? Wait. Not racial slurs . . . species slurs? Anything I should watch out for? *Hey, wolfie!* Would that be super uncool?"

"Yes, but not for the reason you think."

"Har-har. You still haven't answered my question." He had hopped off the bed and was searching for his underwear. "What now? You know. With us. With this. What's next for us? As a couple, I mean." He colored, and she didn't think he was blushing about putting his Batman boxers back on. "Assuming there's an us. Y'know, going forward if we're already an us. But if you didn't think so, it's okay." He was stepping into his jeans and talking faster. "I'm not saying I thought so, or assumed you thought so, but if you did I'd be okay with that."

She tried not to stare as he babbled, but the man looked like he was only seconds from going up in a blaze of spontaneous combustion. It was impossible *not* to stare.

"If you're in it just to have a little fun, I wouldn't . . . I mean, I wouldn't expect—maybe we should just go our separate ways now. Not that I want to! I'm just okay if you want to."

"Wow. Shut up now, okay?"

"Yes ma'am." There was no mistaking the relief in his tone.

"Are you all right? Maybe you should sit down."

"Now that I'm not trying to think and talk at the same time, it's safe for both of us."

"This is new territory for me, too." One of the places they'd lingered was her little shower, which had been too small to have any serious fun, but large enough for considerable foreplay. So she was clean yet rumpled. Not that snoozing in her hobbit hole would have gotten her paws dirty, but habit was strong.

She found clean panties and, for a wonder, a bra the same color. Rachael had nothing but admiration for women who wore matching underwear, but she had never been up to the strain, not to mention the organizational skills. She opened the closet and pulled out a loose, comfortable linen shift in sky blue. *Something to match blue flats . . .*

She pulled the shift over her head. "Some of my girlfriends have dated guys who weren't Pack, but my cousin Michael is the only one I know who took one to mate."

"Yeah? Really? Ooh, I love it, Romeo and Juliet as told by the Pack. His family has too many secrets, and her family Just Doesn't Understand. Together, they—"

"Married quite without problems or interference of any kind, and had two children."

"Story-wise, it's pretty dull. But real-life wise, it's kind of a relief."

She stepped into the bathroom and grabbed a brush. "Our kind—sorry about the term—our kind don't have a problem mating with non-Pack. The cubs—excuse me, the *children* of those matings tend to be exceptional. So of course my cousins are." She grinned as she pulled the brush through her dark locks. "His eldest, Lara, she'll be our next leader, and she's already leading the family through all sorts of trials, you wouldn't even believe it. She's Michael all over again, really, and karma can be a real bitch. She—"

She glanced at Edward, who was listening with rapt attention. "Oh. Sorry, didn't mean to do the my-niece-is-better-than-yours thing."

"Sounds like she is, though! I don't mind. I'd love to hear about everybody in your family. Although I'm punching Michael in the Adam's apple when I meet him. Punk's got a lotta nerve sending you out here like some kind of lycanthropic homing pigeon. *Go here, come there, keep an eye out and make a report* . . . ha!"

"I wouldn't advise punching Michael anywhere, and my point is, there won't be a need for any of that you-can't-stop-our-love! nonsense. Assuming we would even need to go there in the first place. Ah, nuts. I said *go there*. That's officially over now, right? I have to be careful. I don't want to accidentally revive that stupid, stupid saying . . ."

"Okay, I know I fucked up by assuming you were the undead nemesis of all mankind earlier, but I think I earned a couple of points on the positive side when I didn't flee screaming into the night once you popped fur, right?"

"Oh my God."

"Right?"

"*Popped fur?* Really?"

"Shush. But I did, right? You look really, really pretty in that, by the way. Do you have to be somewhere? I've never seen you primp. Maybe I should primp." He widened his eyes and blinked slowly. "You're getting veerrrry sleepy. You want . . . to have . . . more sex. With me!" He blinked harder and slower.

"You look like a hoot owl when you do that. One with a degree in accounting. I'll stop primping if you promise to never primp again. And as far as having to be somewhere, I'm going to return the shoes the vampire queen lent me."

"Awesome! Let me find a shirt and I'll be ready."

"I'm certain my plans for returning footgear to its rightful owner don't include you."

"Too bad! The last time you went there, they threw a knife at your head. Who knows what they'll do next time?"

"Technically they threw the back of a knife at my head. You have to admit, it sounds much less dangerous if you think of it that way."

"Yeah, you can consider me *not* comforted. I'm goin'." He had found his shirt, dark green with white lettering: "I'm Not Unemployed, I'm a Consultant!" "Want to call first? We could call first. Although they apparently don't mind the pop-in. Would you believe her friggin' phone number is on the newsletter? At least, a number she says she can be reached at."

"I saw that as well."

Edward shook his head. "That's no way to run an undead empire. Accessibility? Keeping polite zombies and lending shoes to werewolves while making sure pregnant women get proper prenatal care? The whole thing's too weird and twisted for words."

"Phoning ahead. Hmm. That's not a terrible idea." She'd let Edward call, and while he was killing time playing around with a voice mail account, she could give some thought to the pros and cons of *not* knocking him unconscious and leaving without him.

She was an accountant, and almost any problem, any situation, could be broken down into numbers. So: would letting Edward meet the vampires be good for him or bad for him, and to what degree?

Oh, and the other thing she'd been wondering about: where did he get all those terrific shirts?

Forty-three

"It's ringing!" Edward clutched the phone and kept half an eye on Rachael, who was just too cute for words in her little blue dress. With matching shoes, even. Rachael could look good in a dress made from Filet-O-Fish boxes. "It's ringing. I'm gonna—hello?"

"Hello?"

"Uh, yeah, could I speak to the queen of the vampires? Please," he added. *They probably see being polite as classy, not weak. Right? Hmm. Better hope so.*

"You've got her."

"Oh. Oh! You're her? I mean, it's you?"

"It's me."

"Well, listen good, sweetheart!" He ignored Rachael's

groan. "I don't know what cataclysmic world-killing nefarious plan you have for taking over the world now that I know you're not secretly my girlfriend, but I'm here to tell you it's not gonna happen. I'm gonna make you regret the first dark thought you ever thought! Had, I mean!"

"Is this the host from the Hastings Green Mill?" a pleasant contralto asked.

"Uh, no."

"Satan, then?"

"Really? You think I could be Satan? My voice must be *much* deeper and scarier than I thought." It was wrong to find this terrific fun, right? He never dreamed his voice could be confused with the Lord of Lies.

"Satan is . . . uh . . . yes, the person who is Satan can be very dark and scary, and yes, you do sound a little bit like . . . like the person who is Satan."

This is getting weirder even faster than I thought it would. "Does Satan honestly have your number?" he asked breathlessly. This was the most interesting conversation he'd had in months. "Satan? The Dark Prince himself, he *calls* you?"

For what? Nefarious doings with the queen of the shambling eternally thirsty undead? Playdates? To talk about which movie based on a Marvel superhero or a Disney World ride they would go see together? What? Oh, he had to find out! Actually, if the things he'd heard about the queen were true, she'd probably tell him.

"Seriously, I think that's amazing. I know it's not cool to own that, but I'll admit it: that is seriously cool."

"What is?"

"Satan having your number. He's got it, right? Don't let this all be for nothing. Don't let me get my hopes up like that."

The woman laughed. "The landline, sure. Everybody's got the landline."

"So it's true! This is so typical. The bad guys always act like they've never read a bestseller or seen a movie."

"Bad guys? Now listen here, mister, *I'm* not the bad guy!" The pleasant contralto had a slight midwestern twang. *Now* was *now-oo*, *here* was *hee-er*, *bad* was *bee-ed*. Hilarious! "And I don't appreciate random phone calls from fellas who tell me I *am* the bad guy."

"Don't get huffy. If you don't want random calls, don't list your number in a nationally mailed newsletter. Besides, you *are* the queen of the vampires."

"Okay, yeah, I've got that going against me, but if you over-look that one little thing, you'd see I'm a good guy. Oh . . . who is this, anyway?"

"Listen, despicable vampire queen—"

"Oh, now that's just rude."

"Sorry," he said, immediately chastened. Meanwhile, Rachael had buried her head in her hands and was moaning and rock-ing back and forth like someone trying to find her happy place. He gave her a big smile and flashed her a thumbs-up, but, weirdly, she wasn't comforted. "It's just, I always had a feeling I'd meet you someday, or somebody like you, so I kind of wrote the script for that meeting in my head."

"And I'm not following your script?" she said, sounding like she was cheering up.

"No, not at all," he soothed.

"Really?"

"Oh, we're totally beyond my script. Years beyond."

"Well, okay then." Hmm, the queen of the vampires could turn a frown upside down in no time. "No harm done. What's your name again?"

"I'm Edward B—" Rachael was making slashing-across-the-throat motions. Now she was miming hanging up the phone. Now she was miming strangling him. "Hey, it's none of your business what my name is, Miss Nosy Parker Vampire Queen! But I *am* gonna be stopping by your lair with my hot new werewolf girlfriend, who wants to return some shoes, and we wanted to show we're civilized by calling first. So we're calling first. Bask in how civilized we are. Go on. Bask!"

"*Some shoes* . . . is your hot new werewolf girlfriend a medium-tall brunette? With big brown pansy eyes? And kind of a permanent tight-ass expression until she smiles?"

Wow. "Yeah, but it's more a serious expression than a tight-ass one. Like a sexy librarian."

"I pray she was careful with them."

"You *pray*? With what?" A rosary? Shyeah. A Bible? Ha!

"The shoes! And I'm praying for them, not with them. I've never even met you, but I can already tell you're incredibly weird. Are they okay? She didn't scuff them or step in dog shit or anything, did she?"

"How should I know?" He covered the phone. "The vampire queen wants to know if the shoes are okay."

Rachael, who'd given up with the slashing motions and just stood there listening with an appalled look on her face, nodded. "Sure. They're fine. I've barely worn them. Just to here from her house. And now to her house from here."

"Hear that? The blue thingies are safe and sound."

"They're not thingies. Little boys have thingies. You probably have a thingy."

"Uh . . ." Out of nowhere, the queen's voice had gotten deep and scary.

"Those are Beverly Feldman Bonvivant flats in navy blue."
Little girl from *The Exorcist* deep and scary. "Okay."

"With a satin underlay!"
James Earl Jones deep and scary. "Okay."

"And a cushioned footbed!"

"O-*kay*!" He ignored Rachael's renewed gestures of impending death. "My point was, they're fine. In fact, we're bringing them right over, so just chillax."

"Oh, Edward." Like magic—it was, probably!—the queen's voice was back to the pleasant contralto of earlier. "Nobody says *chillax* anymore."

"Hey, when I need to update my trends and pop culture refs, I'm not gonna check with a vampire. For all I know, you think zoot suits are trendy and you like to relax by doing the Charleston."

"Voh-doh-dee-oh-doh, baby." She laughed. "We're cranking up the blender at four. See ya."

He clicked off the call and looked at Rachael. "She's either super-evil or super-cool."

"Can't she be both?" Rachael rolled her eyes. "You realize after that surreal chat, I have to take you. I'm sure she'll have all kinds of questions. Dammit!"

"Aw, c'mon. It'll be fun."

Rachael had slipped on the blue Beverly Feldman Bonvivant flats and now gave him a look. "Fun? This isn't Dungeons and Dragons, Edward. You could get hurt. You could get dead."

"What about you?"

"They most likely wouldn't dare. They know my cousin sent me out here to keep an eye on things. And they know who my cousin is."

"Yeah, well, they also know who my friend Boo is, so I'm just as well protected—or poorly protected—as you are."

"Careful, Edward. That was almost clever."

"Hey, I'm almost clever lots of times. And now with my hot werewolf gal pal looking out for me? Evil doesn't stand a chance. Besides, if they kill us in horrible grisly protracted ways, Boo will avenge us." He snapped his fingers. "She could be here any hour. If she got a flight out this morning, she could be here any minute. That's the other reason I had to come with. I want to give Boo all the intel I can."

"And you want to give me all the stomach ulcers you can. Come on." She sighed and jerked her head toward the door. "Do you want to walk to our horrible grisly protracted deaths, or drive?"

"Walk. Let's try to keep our deaths as green as we can. Even in death, I try to watch out for planet Earth."

He could tell she didn't want to laugh but couldn't help it. In fact, Rachael laughed so hard she almost fell down on the porch. Which got him started. What with one thing and another, their giggles didn't dry up until they were climbing the steps to the vampire's lair.

If we end up mutilated and murdered, at least we could say we had fun on the way over. It was weird that stuff like that was important to him, right?

Forty-four

"You're going to have to answer some questions," the cop who lived with the vampire queen told them.

Whoa. Edward was still reeling from the intros, never mind the murders. Not that he thought murders should go on anybody's back burner. But a *lot* of shit had been going down lately. Murders just made it grittier.

He was so proud of Rachael . . . she was aces at everything, absolutely everything she did, and playing diplomat with the undead was the least of it.

She'd knocked on the door, cool as you please, and when the zombie answered, she was all, "Hey, how are ya?" and "Have you met my friend Edward?" and "Do you think we could talk to the lady of the house?" All relaxed and polite! Like this was an everyday thing for her!

Which it might be. He had no idea what her life in Massachusetts had been like, but he planned to find out. Because apparently, Cape Cod was *infested* with werewolves! And really, it explained so much . . . all that numb shit people usually put on tourists was probably numb werewolf shit.

Then . . . then! Off they go, and Edward wasn't sure what he was expecting—nothing like a throne room, natch, but something special, like a big fancy living room with thrones instead of sectional couches . . . at the very least, something like that. He was not expecting an industrial-sized kitchen with fruit scattered everywhere and three—three!—blenders cranking out fruit smoothies every ten seconds.

So that's how he ended up drinking a strawberry-banana smoothie with the queen of the vampires and her ilk at five o'clock in the afternoon.

Right, he'd almost forgotten . . . it was only afternoon, but all the vampires were up! None of them knew they were supposed to lie in their coffins and do impersonations of dead people until full dark. They must not be reading the right legends.

Oh, and can we tell the studio audience that the vampire queen's lair is also a COMPLETE BABE FACTORY? Because it is!

First he got a look at the one Rachael had referred to as Jailbait. And yep, she was. Looked it, anyway; God (and maybe the vampire queen) only knew how old she really was. Long blond hair pulled back in a ponytail that ended in the middle of her back. A sleek black headband keeping her bangs out of her eyes. A dark red pleated skirt, spotless white blouse (a good trick in a kitchen that had fruit *everywhere*), red cardigan, spotless white tights, little tiny black flats. And that face! Zow. Pale, perfect, with luminous dark eyes that were almost as pretty as Rachael's.

Yeah. And that was one vampire. *One.*

He'd seen the pregnant woman before, of course, and found out her name was Jessica. It turned out she was one of the only two "normal" ones in the bunch. (Three, if you counted the baby, but who knew what was going to come rocketing out of her?) Except Jessica wasn't just Betsy's friend, she was sort of like Bruce Wayne . . . Edward had gotten the impression that she funded at least some of their operation with her own money.

Oh, and Betsy. Yeah, *Betsy.* That was the name of the queen of the vampires. Yet another illusion, shattered.

"I am pleased to meet Your Dark Majesty," he'd said, all formal and everything (he'd practiced), and the dark majesty started laughing so hard she choked on her smoothie, and Jessica had to bang her on the back four or five times.

When she could talk, she'd greeted him with, "What's it like, being one of the biggest geeks in the world?"

And he'd come back with, "Back off, you harpy. Why don't you go pound some strawberries straight up your nose?"

And she'd liked that. She laughed! And her underlings had laughed, too.

The other normal person turned out to be the father of Jessica's baby . . . and a cop! Edward was filled with admiration. The queen's minions came from all walks of life (and death). Her info pipeline must be as wide as it was deep. Plus, her husband was Dark Dude! And if Dark Dude made less than ten million bucks last year, Edward would eat all the candles on the guy's next birthday cake.

So: rich friends in high and low places, friends with and without pulses, plus her very own zombie army of one (so far).

And that was only what he'd been able to find out in five minutes. He hadn't even tried to find any of that out. He felt lucky to have retained even that info; he was having a *very* hard time keeping from geeking out.

Every time he realized, every time the simple home truth tried to emerge that he was hanging out with vampires (and their queen!) and a werewolf (who he'd had sex with a *lot*!) and a zombie (who was just the nicest guy you could ever meet) and a homicide detective (who not only had knocked up his girlfriend but was fine with his baby growing up in this environment) and someone born during the Civil War (the fucking Civil War!), every time those truths started to emerge, he had to fight the impulse to *utterly geek out.*

Don't you dare. It'll embarrass Rachael. And yourself! And Rachael.

So many questions. So little time. Must . . . squash . . . inner . . . nerd.

So in an attempt to get ahold of himself, to act like an adult, or at least someone so cool they weren't tempted to nerd up during Smoothie Time, in an attempt to somehow bring all that to heel, he'd blurted, "Too bad about all those murders, huh?"

And from there, it had stopped being silly and started being scary.

Forty-five

"This is awkward," Detective Nicholas Berry said, "but you're not a serial killer, are you? Or know any?"

"Not since the operation," Rachael replied. She had liked the homicide detective (*Interest. Curiosity. Lust.*) at once. She didn't hold the frisson of sexual attraction against him. Whether you were Pack or human or undead (or not), you couldn't help it if you were attracted to someone. She never blamed people for that . . . only for how they acted on it.

"What is that, your punch line?" Betsy asked. "You trotted that one out the other day, too. Also not funny, I hesitate to point out, and yet must for the sake of our continued good time."

"Which part wasn't funny, the line, or the fact that she might be a serial killer?"

"Both," the queen admitted. She turned to the detective, a

handsome blond man with swimmer's shoulders and a tan jacket from Armani. *They must pay cops way more in St. Paul than they do in Boston.* They were clearly good friends, judging by the ease in their body language and how they spoke to each other. "What's on your so-called mind, Beriberi?"

"Another nickname, Betsy? Wouldn't it just be easier to get everyone's actual name right? 'Hello, my name is Detective Berry, nice to meet you.' Like that? How hard is that?"

"You do not command me, mortal law enforcer," Betsy had replied with dead-on arrogance, done well enough to make them all snicker. "Go search yourself, Beriberi." Then, to Rachael: "I shouldn't be teasing. Those poor people! And not even killed for something they did. They're just . . . decoration. Killed only because their killer needs something noticed, something that has nothing to do with *them* or the lives they led."

In that moment, Rachael liked the vampire queen more than she could have imagined. She had assumed a vampire queen would have the standard arsenal of charisma and charm. She hadn't expected that respect would follow so quickly on the heels of liking.

"What are you talking about?" Edward was looking at both of them. "Did you find something out?"

"You could say that," Detective Berry said. "DNA."

"No shit! Then you've got him, right?"

The detective smiled at Edward, but it was a nice smile, and there wasn't a trace of condescension in his voice when he replied, "It's not quite as simple as *Law and Order* makes it out to be."

"Those bastards lied to us *again*?" Jessica yelped. "Oh, Detectives Stabler and Benson, say it ain't so."

"Oh, God, don't start on those two," Edward groaned. "My roommate—one of my roommates—lives for that show. He's got a huge crush on Mariska Hargitay. He went to see an episode of *The Martha Stewart Show* because she was the guest star and Martha taught her how to make doilies, or something."

Rachael had noticed the other vampire—*not* the queen—had flinched at *oh, God*. That was good to know. That was very good to know.

"Well, anyway, the murders aren't in our jurisdiction, but Betsy's boss man, there, made a few phone calls."

"Eric Sinclair is not my boss man," the queen said, every word a knife.

"Easy, whoa there, big fella," Jessica said. "Take it easy, Betsy. Your pills?"

"Well, he's not."

"The DNA didn't hit."

"So it wasn't any good?" Rachael asked. She was privately wondering if there was any way she or Mrs. Cain could get to a crime scene and give it a sniff.

"I didn't say it wasn't any good. I said it didn't hit. Lucky for you, huh, Rachael?"

She blinked. They were all looking at her, even Edward. "What?" *Concern. Fear. Worry. Concern. Resignation.* "What's wrong?"

"It's your DNA, Rachael."

Forty-six

"Whoa!"

"Edward—"

"Whoa, whoa, whoa, whoa!" Edward had more than jumped out of his seat. He had rocketed out of the damned thing. Adrenaline was a wonderful thing.

He'd jumped up and run over and stood in front of Rachael. "She didn't do it!"

"We know."

"So just pack up your arresting paperwork and back off, Beriberi!"

"Oh, don't tell me that stupid nickname's gonna stick now."

"Focus, please! Someone's out to make Rachael look bad. Like they even *could*, I mean, *look* at the woman. They don't come much hotter than this, right?" He gestured to her. She hadn't moved from her seat, just shifted her weight so she could tip her head back and look straight at him. "That's what all this has been about, making vampires look bad to Pack, and Pack look bad to vamps."

"That was our theory as well."

"There's no way she went to any of those crime scenes and committed any of those murders to make those crime scenes. *No* way!"

"Edward—"

"Shut up, Rache," he muttered. Then, louder, "You guys don't even know, okay? She's as smart as she is hot, but even better, she's as nice as she is smart. Do you know how rare it is to find a chick *this* smokin' who isn't also a huge bitch? Huh? Because it's pretty fucking rare!"

"Awwww," the queen said. Then: "He's right. We *are* rare."

"She's not out here by choice, she got *sent* here, like for a job. She was made to yank her entire life out by the roots and drag it halfway across the country, get it? And she's such a good person she didn't question any of it! So now here she is, and bodies are piling up, and that's not her fault and it's probably not even you guys' fault, but here she is anyway, stuck in the middle of a mess she didn't make. But she's here, right? Getting shit done. She got sent to keep an eye on you guys . . . and you land her in this kind of trouble? When she could have said *fuck you* to all of us and stayed home?"

He knelt beside her, took her hand in his—

worry anger fear anger love love love love worry anger love love love

—and said, "Rache, I know you'd never do anything like this. These guys aren't touching you. Nobody's laying a finger on you, got it? We'll get you out of here and you'll call your cousin and he'll fix everything or you'll engage your awesome brain and solve the crime.

"But I'm not letting them put you in a cage for even one nanosecond. I know you guys—the Pack . . . well, I don't know the Pack. I only know you. And you couldn't stand being in a cage. Not even a dinky holding cell downtown for a couple of hours. And as long as I'm here—"

"Encouraging you to add *resisting arrest* to your résumé," Detective Berry said dryly.

"—nobody's gonna lock you away."

"Edward . . ."

"I mean it, Rache."

"Edward, you're a fool."

"Thanks, I lo—wait. You aren't saying the lines I imagined you'd say," he admitted, looking flustered.

"You're a fool and I love you."

"Oh. I imagined you saying something like that, even if you're not saying it exactly the way I pictured."

"I'd like to take you for my mate. I'd like to bear your cubs."

He looked at her. He looked and his eyes got bigger and

bigger and she was getting a little alarmed—would he pass out?—when he turned away from her and said to the room, "Y'see? She loves me! And I love her! (I've just realized.)" He turned to her. "You knew I loved you before I did. This is one of those cool werewolf things where you knew something about me I didn't know!"

"That isn't true, Edward." She kissed him, a long one full of what they both knew. "You knew before your body could give me the cues. Otherwise, there wouldn't have been anything for me to pick up on."

He quickly kissed her back. "I love you."

"Yes, I know."

"Are you really gonna be smug about this?"

"Sure."

He laughed, and then remembered they wanted to arrest his lover—except was she now his fiancée, maybe?—for multiple murders.

Right. Back to work.

Forty-seven

"Right! Okay." He took a few seconds to get his bearings. "So, in closing, don't you dare even waste half a minute arresting mah woman—I always wanted to try pronouncing it like that—when she's not guilty. *Mah* woman!"

Edward was watching the others carefully; he was the only one standing. Not even the cop had stood. They were just sort of sprawled in their chairs around the table, sipping smoothies and watching him.

Good. Maybe they were going to stay cool. That'd be unexpected and lovely. Nothing like this had ever happened to him before. Worse, nothing like this had ever been written about in a movie or graphic novel or book before, as far as he knew, so he had no idea where to go from there.

"Rachael, Detective Beriberi said it himself, it's not even his jurisdiction. So you and I are going to get up and walk out of here and then you're gonna call your cousin and get the cavalry out here to find the real killer—"

"We're pretty sure we know who that is," Detective Berry said, "so if you need a name or address, just let me know."

"—so you can clear your name." *Wait. What?* "Wait. What?"

"Well, let's see. If you have a name, that means not only did you find my DNA," Rachael guessed, "you found proof that it was planted DNA. Something I couldn't have left behind by accident. And since I wouldn't go to the trouble of planting my own DNA at a crime scene when I'm a good source of my own DNA, you knew someone was trying to frame me."

"Hey, that sounds pretty good . . . hmmm." Okay. Well, he knew Rachael was as smart as she was hot. Good to have further verification on that. "Uh, what have you guys all figured out that I don't know yet?" It was gonna sound vain, but he was sort of used to being the smartest person in the room, in most rooms . . .

"I didn't figure anything out," the queen said, looking sympathetic. "Honest. They had to explain it to me, too."

It worked! He smiled at her and said, "Hey, thanks, that actually cheered me up. I've been standing here wondering how long I need to keep the dunce cap on."

"The DNA was Rachael's," the detective said. "But it had been planted by someone who isn't that good at such things."

"Fingerprints, maybe moved with something like Scotch tape?" Rachael guessed.

"How the hell do you even know that?" Edward demanded.

"Because I forgot and then forgot I forgot."

"In English, *por favor*?"

"I left my travel guide in her office."

"Whose?"

"Mrs. Cain's. The woman at the chamber of commerce. The one who got things ready when she knew I was coming. The one who set me up for murder. The one who lifted my DNA from anything in her office I'd touched and brought it to crime scenes and"—Rachael spread her hands and looked wry—"spread the wealth."

"But . . ." He looked around. The rest of them looked just as blank as he felt. "But why?"

"I don't know." Rachael moved—flowed, almost—to her feet. If he'd blinked, he would have missed it. Girl could *move* when she wanted to. "But I'm going to go ask her."

Forty-eight

"It's over, you know."

Mrs. Cain sighed. "Yes. I know."

"Even if you hadn't called, I'd have come for you."

"I know. I didn't think it would really work. I told him that."

Rachael's head began to throb in time with her heartbeat. "But you did it anyway, Mrs. Cain. You did it *anyway*."

The older woman's head came up proudly. Rachael had never seen her in casual clothes: black jeans and an orange long-sleeved T-shirt. Athletic socks. Tennis shoes. "I was asked. They were family. What else could I have done?"

"Oh, I don't know. Maybe not committed *multiple murders*?"

"You should see the smug look on your face right now. Pretending if your precious Michael asked you to kill, pretending it'd turn out any different."

I am dealing with a crazy person. "If that's what you want to think."

"It isn't what I *want* to think," Rachael flashed. She'd crossed her small living room in half a blink, more than a little annoyed she'd allowed this person into her den. "It's what *is.* I didn't call you to sit in judgment."

"Then why did you?" The time. She had to be careful of the time. Edward would miss her soon. Worse: the queen might. She did *not* want the queen of the vampires anywhere near Pack business. Bad enough that Cain had pointed fingers that led vampires this far . . . and hopefully no further.

"I must know. I felt I—we—had been careful."

"He wasn't careful at all. And you knew that." She tilted her head, studying the other woman. "What an odd time to start lying."

"I was never much good at it."

"Don't be so hard on yourself," she said dryly. "You covered pretty well before . . . half-truths got you through it. If you were tense about the murders, you saw me when you could explain how you were tense about something else." The new ad campaign. Deadlines. An old Pack trick, but a good one— scents can't lie, but you can misrepresent their source.

"It was the only thing I could think to do."

"When you were pissed I was going to see the vampire queen, you discussed it when I would assume you were pissed over a possible scuffle for territory. You were mad; I knew you were. But you were mad because trying to make friends with the vampires was not the plan. If your goal was to sow mistrust, the *last* thing you wanted was open communication between their people and ours."

"You have a reputation for being standoffish," Mrs. Cain said sharply. "Frankly, it never occurred to me that you would be so sociable."

"I'm thrilled to disappoint you."

Cain muttered something that sounded like *itch*. (It probably wasn't *itch*.)

"You knew I'd smell a lie on you . . . so each time you had to lie, you made sure you had an explanation."

Cain just looked at her for a long moment. *Annoyance. Shame. Irritation.* "Yes, which brings me back to my question . . . how did you know I was involved?"

"Who *else* would it have been, Cain? I've been in town less than two weeks, and besides my landlords and Edward, you're the only one I know here."

"Except for the vampires," she snapped.

The time. Keep an eye on the time. "The pool of suspects was quite shallow." *Murder mysteries are never like this. There's usually more than one suspect. Ah, now I'm sounding like Edward . . . clearly, I fell for the hype.* If the whole murderous mess hadn't been so wasteful and tragic, she would have been amused. "You created a list of people for me to meet. Then you helped your man kill his way through the list. Then you dumped them in the Summit Avenue area . . . what a Pack member would consider vampire territory. Even better, what a *vampire* would consider vampire territory.

"You knew I'd be right in the middle of it all, keeping an eye on the vampires and unwittingly keeping things stirred up. When the queen looked into the murders happening so near, she'd wonder what had changed. I was the change. A Pack member, set right in the dead center of her territory. And with things between our people and hers still in a bit of an uproar . . . well. It wouldn't have taken much to set off those fireworks. And I'd be gone . . . killed by a vamp, maybe. Or arrested by a human . . . which would bring my name to their attention. Word would also get back to Michael. And there'd be a mess. A big fat mess in the last place any of us wanted it.

"And once the hurricane whipped through our lives, you'd have what you wanted."

"Yes."

"Except you couldn't. Because you killed him. Didn't you?"

A long silence, finally broken by her sigh. "Yes. I had to. He'd shamed the family. He'd endangered the Pack."

She's gone insane. Absolutely flipped her lid. I should feel worse for her than I do. What a waste! All of it, pure waste! Oh God, God, what was it all FOR?

"I didn't do anything wrong."

That was so absurd, Rachael had no idea what to say. *There's something very wrong with this woman.* And then, of course, she realized what it was. *I should feel sorry for you. I don't, though. I guess . . . I'm a bad person after all.*

"I didn't," she repeated.

"You did, actually. And you're not even a bad guy."

She actually smiled at that. "No?"

"No, Cain, you're not *a* bad guy." Rachael spoke gently, with what little pity she could manage. "You're the worst kind of bad guy. You *think* you're the good guy. So in your mind, every terrible deed is justified for the greater good. It's why you're so dangerous. It's why my cousin will most likely kill you."

"To come kill me? Here?" She laughed, a grating and ugly noise. "What, and leave his precious Cape Cod and his precious monkey wife—"

"Cain!" Rachael's usually mild temperament left her; her shout was part growl, part roar. *Monkey* was a vicious pejorative to describe their brothers who had evolved on the far side of the world. It was just about the worst slur a werewolf could use. "Watch your filthy mouth!"

"Oh. I see." Cain's upper lip was curling and lifting, curling and lifting, showing Rachael quick flashes of sharp, white teeth. It was unconscious but spoke volumes. *Anger. Anger. Anger. Anger.* "You've met one. You're fucking one. I can smell him on you."

"I doubt it. Most likely you're smelling yourself. When *was* the last time you showered?"

"Traitor."

"You're not going to do the sad and stupid our-bloodline-must-be-kept-pure nonsense, right? First off, it's not true, and second, it's just so pathetic. Please, please . . . if you've got a gun, shoot me in the face." Not as nasty as *monkey*, but a sly shot all the same. Using anything but teeth and claws to kill was considered lazy and contemptible. "Shoot me in the face, the knee, throw me under your car and then back up a few times, whatever, just don't start with the race-traitor crap. Because I can't think of anything sillier to discuss."

"Well, you are one! You're the one running around banging monkeys."

"More than that, even," she said, staying calm. *This woman is insane. You know why. You know what's wrong with her. It doesn't excuse anything . . . but it bears keeping in mind. Don't rise again. Don't.* "I'm taking him for a mate."

"Other than trying to induce me to vomit in your wastebasket, why would you ever tell me that?" Lift. Curl. Lift. Curl.

"So I can see your face when I explain that he's ten times the person you'll ever be, Cain. He wouldn't set up an innocent for murder. He wouldn't sit back while bystanders were targeted and killed because he got *homesick*. And he'd never turn on family . . . he wouldn't kill the killer."

"Oh, yes, please tell me more. It's so fascinating to me. The monkeys are *so* civilized."

"Only compared to some. But what I'd really like to know, Cain, the reason I bothered to come back here at all . . ." *The reason I sent Edward and the queen on a wild monkey chase . . .* "Why? You must tell me, because that's what eats at me (so to speak). Your motive. You've never done anything like this before, correct? And that's what troubles me. Settled middle-aged office employees don't just suddenly plan, aid, and abet felony murder. So what happened? Why now?"

Anger. Shame. Anger. Anger. Anger.

"Because they're my cousins," Cain said, her expression making clear she thought it was a stupid question. "They're family."

"Yeah." She sighed. "I was afraid it was something like that. Cousins."

"Their business is their life. It's everything to them."

"And I was in the way."

"You were in the way."

"You didn't need me to be convicted, or even tried. Just inconvenienced enough to muddy the waters." *Over an audit? Of all the stupid, pointless . . .*

"It was working. You were out there, like a goat staked for bait. You weren't—you shouldn't have—"

Made allies of the people who were supposed to condemn her. *Yes, I can see how that would really screw up your plan.*

"Aren't you ashamed?" She could hear how plaintive she

sounded. It was the sort of question a child asked, but Rachael couldn't help it. When she thought of the wasted lives, she wanted to weep. "All this mess, and for what? For nothing, in the end."

"For everything. For my family."

When Cain went for her, Rachael was ready. Almost relieved, really. Not that one could ever really be ready for a fight to the death, but Rachael had walked through the door knowing there was a 94.62 percent chance she would have to fight for her life if she ever wanted to leave her den under her own power, rather than hitching a ride in a body bag.

So Cain dived across the desk, the small quaint rolltop desk that had seen more action in the last seven days than in the last seven years, and Rachael managed to avoid the woman's grasping, clawing hands. She was more than a little relieved. She was an accountant, not a warrior, and it was good to see the woman was much slower than she was.

Cain recovered quickly and slashed at Rachael, forcing her back. "Can't you try to have some dignity here at the end?"

"What"—grope, slash—"do you think"—claw, grab— "this *is*?"

"Pathetic. That's what I think this is." But Rachael was relieved, too. She hadn't really wanted to fight to the death. She was fine with merely overpowering the woman and turning her over to either the envoy of Michael's choice or the local police, who would—

—be delighted to find the murder weapon. Which Cain had

brought with her to Rachael's hobbit hole. *Shamed, yes, but not nearly enough. Should have foreseen that, yes you should have, and you'll pay for your arrogance now, won't you, you silly bitch?*

"You brought the gun?" Cain's hands had gone to the small of her back and *now*, yes, *now* Rachael could smell gun oil, now that Cain was lifting her shirt and bringing the weapon out to bear, now she could smell it, but *now* was going to be too late, and she had no one to blame but herself. "You brought a *gun* into my den? You actually *brought* one of those things into my *den*, you faithless bitch?"

She would be too slow, and her only consolation was that she'd kept Edward out of it. Edward was safe. Yes, he was—

There.

"No!" she screamed. "Oh, no, don't, don't, don't come in, don't you dare come in!"

But he did dare.

Forty-nine

"I don't know who Rachael thinks she's kidding with all this meet-me-all-the-way-across-town-in-half-an-hour bullshit," Edward informed the king of the vampires. "It's so obvious she's going to go to her place to either look for the chamber lady, or is setting up a meeting so the chamber lady comes to the hobbit hole where all will be revealed . . . something stupid and brave and really illogical."

Eric Sinclair, beloved of Betsy and king of the undead, grinned. Edward had to make an actual, conscious effort not to flinch from that look. "Brave and really illogical would accurately describe Her Majesty."

"And a lover of all things smoothie."

The king chuckled, a sound that was somehow light and dark at the same time. "Yes. That, too."

"Thanks for helping me split them up."

"Not at all. I prefer my queen to be half a city away from possible felony assault. And she takes justifiable pride in knowing she can go out into the world earlier in the day than I can. So it was a fine thing, letting her leave first."

He'd *thought* that was kind of weird but had decided not to say anything yet. But yeah, *Betsy* could go outside while it was still light out. *Sinclair* couldn't. He had to wait until it was almost full dark, like now.

Edward pointed at his chest as they rolled silently into the driveway for the hobbit hole. "Knew it. Totally called it. You asked Betsy and Tina and Beriberi to go where you're pretty sure the bad guy *isn't*."

"It was not a question of pretty sure."

"No?"

"No. The killer is there right now."

"Wait, you knew she'd be at her office downtown?"

Sinclair just looked at him. Edward almost heard the *click* as he got it: "You *knew* she'd be here, laying here for Rachael in her very own hobbit hole! Oooh, your wife's gonna be soooo pissed at you!"

"I am aware, Edward."

"You'll be on Sofa Sentry for months!"

"*I am aware, Edward.*"

"All right, sheesh, calm down. So what's the plan?"

"You stay here while I suavely save the day."

"Yes, and here on Planet Real Life, what's the plan?"

But then things got unpleasant really, really fast, because King Sinclair said, "Gun." (Everybody called him Sinclair, even his wife!) And all Edward could do was run in after him and hope he was somehow in time or, barring that, that he could somehow help.

As it turned out, no one needed his help.

The king of the vampires had rushed in fast enough to knock the gun away without doing any real damage to a frowsy, middle-aged woman in an orange T-shirt. But Orange T-shirt wasn't inclined to meekly surrender, because she was going for Rachael.

And Rachael! Rachael had a look of fury on her face that Edward had never seen on anyone, ever. He had time for a confused thought/prayer (*please don't let me be dumb enough to ever make her that mad*).

Then Rachael was reaching for Orange T-shirt, and Orange T-shirt was reaching for Rachael with just as much hatred and intensity on her face, and for a second everything was all sharp teeth and razor-sharp nails and blurred limbs and then Rachael . . . Rachael grabbed her. Dragged her. She—

Edward had to think about it and, though it happened right in front of him, he didn't have senses that had evolved in a way for him to take in every point of action. So after he had thought about it for a while in his careful, planning, tool-making mind, he realized what he had seen.

Orange T-shirt, reaching. Rachael, also reaching . . . and grabbing, and seizing, and hauling the other woman hard and fast, dragging her across the desk and then lifting her in the air and slamming her back down, only she slammed the woman's head on the edge of the desk; Rachel shoved her down so hard and so fast her neck broke instantly with a crack Edward would hear, on and off, in nightmares for the rest of his life.

Rachael had broken the woman's neck on the edge of the desk, and done such a thorough job that when the woman's ass hit the carpet, she was already dead.

"Um . . . look out?" he managed. The vampire king was holding the murder weapon the way he'd hold a dead garter snake. *Better remember to tell him to wipe his fingerprints off. Maybe he's got his own secret police to worry about stuff like that.* "We're here to save you?"

"Oh, my, now look at this," the king said mildly, but he was giving Rachael a sharp look, one with more than a little approval. "*That* was unexpected."

"It was my right." Rachael was breathing hard. Edward realized the woman was actually shaking. "She defiled my den, where my mate sleeps. It was my right. She defiled our den. Where he *sleeps.* It was my right, Edward. It was my right."

"Sure it was, Rache. I know. She had a lot of nerve, huh? It's all right."

Trembling, a Rachael he had never seen before crept into his arms. She was shaking so hard he had a little trouble holding her at first. "If she would bring it when you weren't here, she'd bring it when you *were*." Rachael made a small sound, like a dry sob. "Oh, Edward, what if you'd been here when she brought that thing?"

"Never happen, not with Rachael Velveeta on the case. Listen, when you're done having your nervous breakdown, can I have mine? Because I just watched you kill someone in a really awesome way, and although it's a good thing, I think, it's also freaking me out."

"Okay, but I get to go first."

"Naturally."

"And my turn's not done yet. Please hold me and make those dumb soothing noises like you do."

He was happy to comply. Edward assumed that was some kind of Pack rule of thumb, the being-safe-while-sleeping concept. He was slowly beginning to understand that Rachael hadn't killed Orange T-shirt in the heat of battle, or even in the cold glow of vengeance. She'd killed Orange T-shirt out of fear for *his* safety. She'd killed Orange T-shirt to protect him, the same as she would have for the kids they would someday have.

He supposed he should have been scared and worried, but he was too filled with pride, and his pride and his love were too big for any other emotion right now.

Being able to sleep soundly while not getting shot at must be a really big deal to the Pack, he decided. He also decided that it was an excellent rule for him, too. He didn't have to ask if Rachael was on board.

"Well, well."

Edward had forgotten all about the vampire king, who had seen everything but had very little to say, which Edward was starting to think was a standard thing with this guy. "This will be interesting. I very much like interesting." King Sinclair smiled and, in the gloom, white teeth flashed. "Welcome to the neighborhood."

Fifty

"Is your husband still—"

"On Sofa Sentry? He told me your Edward called it that. I love it. It's perfect. And yeah, bet your ass he is."

Your Edward. Rachael liked the sound of that. Lots. She lifted a hand to wave at Call Me Jim, who had just now come onto the porch. Edward was stretched out on the sofa, his head in her lap, reading the few clippings that covered the murders, which, to the public, had stopped as mysteriously and seemingly motive-free as they had begun. Given that Cain had been walking and talking (and lying, and killing) just a couple hours ago made this peaceful scene sort of reek unreality. But she wasn't going to question it.

"Listen, Betsy, I just have to know—"

"It couldn't wait for two hours from now?"

"If I have to suck down one more smoothie I'm going to vomit raspberries for the better part of the week. Enough with the smoothies. You will not see me during Smoothie Time tonight. What I've been wondering about is that damned news-letter."

"Yeah?"

"Yeah. This all started because you put your address in a newsletter, which you then mailed to strangers all over the country."

The queen laughed. "You make it sound like a bad thing."

"I'd hoped I was making it sound like a thing I didn't under-stand."

"Yeah, I get that. You know I haven't been the queen very long, right?"

"I might have heard a few things."

"Mmmm. The CliffsNotes version is, I had to indirectly kill the last idiot who thought he was royalty of the undead. Which sent up a *huge* red flag to pretty much anyone worried about a vitamin D deficiency. There's a new queen in town, watch out! Holy shit, what are we gonna do? Like that, right?

"My husband wanted to hide in plain sight, behind a . . . what weirdo way did he describe—oh! Hide behind a shield of fear and intimidation. Like when Walmart brings out the law-yers. That's what he wanted to do, and I came to see the sense of it.

"Because let's face it . . . once I created a vacancy and immediately (yet reluctantly) filled it, someone was always going to be coming after me. Fucking *always*. It was totally inevitable. We could have bet our lives on it. We *did* bet our lives on it, come to think of it. So, knowing that, accepting that, we put our contact info right out there. There was nothing we could have done to prevent someone from gunning for us. But we could do plenty about how the regime change was perceived. So! A newsletter. Hi, I'm Betsy, glad to be part of the team, looking forward to meeting you, come on by anytime, blah-blah-blah."

"Sending the message that you in your new role are so powerful, you don't care if other vampires can find you." Rachael had to admire the audacity. If someone killed her cousin to run the Pack, and made a point of being extremely findable afterward, she knew she would instantly rethink strategy. She would assume the new guy *wanted* to be found, was making a point of it, which made the whole thing smell like a trap. "In fact, you *want* other vampires to find you. To pay homage or just acknowledge your sovereignty and . . . and . . . what do they do?"

"Drop off bags of blood oranges." The queen sighed. "Regular oranges symbolize the death of Christ. Blood oranges symbolize the rise of the new ruler, the one who rules after Christ and will for thousands of years. Which, um, is me."

"Okay."

"I know how it sounds."

"Okay."

"Because first of all, gross, *blood* oranges? What scary-ass universe did *those* come from? And second, lame. And third, lame. But! That's the newsletter story. And hey! I never did get those shoes back from you."

"Sorry, I was busy with my first-ever kill."

"Oh, jeez, Roberta!"

"Rachael." *It's uncanny how the woman is so bad at names.*

"Yeah, I know, I was just testing you. How long are you gonna flog that as an excuse? 'Boo-hoo, I had to shed Pack blood in defense of my den, yadda-yadda.' You're lucky you broke her neck, because if she'd bled on those shoes, you and I would be having a very different conversation right now. You know, I got those at a sample sale? And normally I don't like sample sales, because I think it sets up an unfair advantage . . ."

This woman is either brilliant or deranged. And either way, she's got good people, which for a leader is more than half the battle.

Brilliant.

"—like anyone could just pop into the store and buy them straight off the rack like that! 'No way,' I said. You can't—"

No. Deranged.

"—get outta town with that shit! Of course, he got all kinds of pissy when I knocked him off the roof. He only fell six stories and the parking ramp broke his fall, so I don't—"

No. Brilliant.

Fifty-one

"Wait, wait, wait. She went crazy? Mrs. Cain just up and went bonzo nutso and arranged for someone to start killing random strangers and that's it? That's the explanation? Because that sucks, Rache. Bad enough it's about *audits*." Edward turned to Nick Berry. "You believe that? Audits. I'm an accountant, and I still almost don't believe it."

"Almost?"

"Mmmmm . . . audits can be pretty nasty. But still . . . man, have some perspective!"

She nodded. "I know, honey. When you put innocent lives up against cold numbers, it doesn't seem just wasteful. Sinful, if you'll pardon an old-fashioned reference."

"A classic," Detective Berry said. When told of Rachael's

smoothie boycott, the laid-back cop had taken a stroll over to the hobbit hole to tie up the loose ends he'd been mulling over.

Rachael hadn't been at all surprised. In fact, she'd been counting on it . . . Call Me Jim had met Berry at the door with a plate of peanut butter brownies. The pitcher of ice cold milk hadn't hurt, either.

Now he was on the sherbet porch, wolfing down brownies and peppering her with questions. Even though it wasn't his jurisdiction, a cop was a cop. And every one Rachael had met had curiosity bumps the size of railroad cars.

"Wait. Wait. Wait." Nick had stuffed the last of the brownie in his mouth and was holding up both hands like a cop who has just realized he can't control rush hour in Boston. "Let's get back to the motive, please. This whole thing. This sinister conspiracy? The murders? Getting Rachael sent to the wilds of Minnesota—"

"St. Paul has a population of about three hundred thousand," Rachael corrected mildly. "I don't think *wilds* is the right word. And despite how it looks, Michael chose me to come out here. No one influenced his decision. Sometimes a cigar is just a cigar."

"—was all so two guys no one but you ever met could avoid an *audit*?"

Rachael nodded. "Makes sense."

Nick rounded on her even as he snaked another brownie

off the plate. "*What?* These things are gonna kill me. You eat like this all the time? Will your landlords let me move in, too? And again: *what?*"

"Well, it does make sense, from a numbers perspective. You've never sat through an IRS audit."

"I guess I shouldn't be surprised. I've been in homicide for years. Except I am," he admitted. "I am surprised. I am very surprised. Murder to avoid an audit."

She smiled at the earnest blond in the Cole Haan jacket. "I think it's nice that you're surprised."

"Oh, me, too," Edward said, backing her up.

"In a pathetic way. In the way that I no longer think of you as a real man because you could be surprised by this."

"You understand I can just start writing tickets on your rental right now? While I'm eating brownies?"

"Brown shirt thug."

"So the guys you saw before you moved out here. They were trying to buy your client's company."

"Yes."

"So they audited the bejeezus out of it. But in order to make the acquisition, their own numbers were gonna get flogged, too."

"Correct." *Flogged.* She'd have to remember that one.

"Which would have exposed all sorts of numbers nastiness. Stealing company funds, stealing from clients, all that good shit."

"Yes. And because they knew I'd insist on doing the audit . . ."

And she would have. Oh, yes. She still remembered their sneaky-nasty looks, their greasy smiles. "I would have audited the shit out of them."

"Oh my God." Edward clutched her hand. "I just fell in love with you all over again. That was so hot. Say *audited the shit out of them* again, but this time do it topless. Beriberi, get lost."

"So they reached out," he continued, doing his best to ignore Edward (which he knew from experience was nigh impossible), "to their cousin, right here in St. Paul: Mrs. Cain. And she came up with the people to kill, and how to implicate you and, even better, how to stir up more anti-vampire/Pack crap. One of them flew in from the Cape for the murders. And she was in a pretty good position to know how the investigation was going as well as how things were going between you and the vampires."

"Yes."

"But . . ." The detective chewed for a while and said nothing.

Edward, who'd had his head in Rachael's lap, sat up. "It doesn't seem like enough, does it, dude?" he asked, kindly enough.

"Yeah. I get why they were killed, but I'm not seeing Mrs. Cain's metamorphosis from office manager to contract-killer-by-proxy."

No, he wouldn't; he wasn't Pack. But for her love, she would try to explain as she had to Edward.

"If it helps, Mrs. Cain was what I consider to be clinically insane. It . . . it probably didn't seem like it to you. It wouldn't seem like it to a lot of people. But she'd been out here for so long . . .

"Sometimes, if we're separated from our Pack for too long, it exacerbates a condition that can form over time . . . there's something wrong with us. At the fundamental level. Your people are much, much better suited to survival than we are. You *vastly* outnumber us."

Though he'd heard most of this before, she knew Edward was paying close attention. It sounded odd to her, using words like *your people*. She had so rarely thought about Pack vs. non-Pack in her old life. That was a habit she must change, and she was glad of it, even as she was a little intimidated.

Edward will help me. We'll help each other.

"I think . . . I think part of the reason your kind thrive is because you're missing that fundamental thing. The distance . . . the loneliness . . . it's something that gets worse if we're alone. Mrs. Cain basically came down with the Pack version of cabin fever. Except ours is based almost entirely on being homesick, or even just lonely. Not for nothing is our strongest urge to mate for life and have as many cubs as we can!"

"Wow, mate for life, huh?" Berry said, straight-faced. "Score."

"Tell me." Edward held out his knuckle for a bump from the detective.

"Hilarious, you two. But back to Mrs. Cain . . . she got more and more lonesome out here, more and more isolated. When that happens, our judgment goes right into the toilet. After *that*, it gets much harder to tell right from wrong. The condition . . . it feeds on itself, do you understand? It's like a Michael Crichton novel . . . one little thing goes wrong and suddenly the dinosaurs can open doors. People have . . ." She spread her hands, a helpless expression on her face. "Well. People have died."

"Jesus." Edward was horrified and didn't trouble himself to hide it. "That's awful. That poor woman."

"Don't feel too sorry for her. She had options."

"I wasn't going to throw her a parade, don't worry. And I'd never try to say I understood something that seems to prey pretty hard on Pack people. But maybe I can relate a little. I wasn't exactly super-thrilled to come out here."

"No? It seemed to me to be much more your idea to come than someone else's for you to leave."

"Yeah, but consider the someone elses! I left because I finally realized I was afraid to leave. And I was afraid to leave because I was afraid they'd—Boo and Greg—let me go. I knew I'd be the pathetic roomie who forces connections when you're not roommates anymore. The guy who never, ever lets you off his Xmas list and who, when he's in town to visit, insists on lunch and pretends you're still really close. I couldn't face it, not any of it, so I stayed. And stayed, and stayed. I'm an object at rest that loves remaining at rest."

"You think *you* didn't want to leave?" Rachael asked. "Try

being raised in a Pack society with mega-strict hierarchies and being *told* to leave."

"Sounds sucky," he agreed. "Say, you're not one of those people who feel compelled to one-up every story you hear, are you?"

"I absolutely am. I can never resist. It's a huge compulsion for me."

"I've never hated someone I've loved so much . . . Listen, so Mrs. Cain, she just cracked up? From being so lonesome and missing the Pack? What if that happens to you?"

"It's rare."

"So? I don't want something awful and rare to happen to you. If we need to move to Werewolf 90210, or whatever the hell you guys call it, then we'll move. We'll move tonight if you want."

"I'm fine, idiot. I was explaining something that happens very occasionally under horrific circumstances. We don't need to rent a U-Haul right this minute. Oh, that reminds me. I'll be in season this time next week, so when we have sex, I'll probably get pregnant. We should keep that in mind when we're looking for a permanent residence. I love my hobbit hole, but it would be crowded for two, never mind three."

"And on *that* note," Berry said, rising, "I think I'll head out. Thanks for your time. Oh, and thank Mr. . . . nuts, he told me his name, but I—"

"Call me Jim," he said, stepping on the porch. "You gotta leave now?"

"Well," Berry said, eyeing the plate of brownies so fresh out of the oven they steamed, "not right this very second . . ."

"It's nice when stuff can get wrapped up like that, huh?" Edward said.

"I'm not sure I consider this *stuff* wrapped up. But a few explanations are better than none at all, I guess. At least we—"

Edward sat bolt upright, horrified. "What? What?" Rachael tried to look in five directions at once.

"Boo! I forgot all about Boo! She's trying to get a flight out here and I haven't called or checked my phone or—oh, fuck! Oh, she's gonna kill me. Oh, shit, I'm dead. I am a walking, talking corpse. Except not a vampire. Or a zombie. No, they're the lucky ones when you compare them to what she's gonna do to me. Ah, jeez, I told her all about Marc the zombie and . . . oh, fuck!"

"What's a boo?" Berry asked thickly, reaching for another glass of milk.

Epilogue

"You want to explain to me why there's a "Sold" sign in my landlord's front yard?"

"Really?" Her cousin's voice on the phone, deep and amused. "You need an explanation? You can't make that deductive leap all by your lonesome?"

"Michael . . ."

"Because that would make you a terrible accountant."

"Michael!"

"Well, it would."

She ground her teeth. "There was never a 'For Sale' sign, so how could it even be sold?"

"Before you even went out there, when I talked to Cain and Cain talked to them, they'd discussed wanting to sell their family home—too big for them for years—so they could retire more and move to North Dakota."

"That makes *no* sense."

"Oh, sure it does, what with the real estate market being in such a slump. They were smart not to bother listing until the market began to recover." Then, softly, to someone else: "Two minutes, honey. Then Daddy will push you on the swing. Gotta finish with cousin Rachael." Louder: "Lara says hi and she loves you."

"You know what I mean, you deliberate goob, and tell Lara I love her, too. And what is this *retire more*? And who retires in any capacity in order to end up, on purpose, in North Dakota?"

"The way I got it from Cain—may she rest in peace or burn in hell as long as she's gone forever—these two aren't very good at retiring."

"They've made a lot of pies in the two weeks I've been here," Rachael admitted.

"So they wanted to retire *more*, and build their dream home in the most beautiful place they knew, which happens to be in the state of North Dakota beside the lake where they'd honeymooned.

"After Cain was out of the picture and I heard that, I found out what fair market value was for their home and made a cash offer, which they took. They never even had to list their house. Which, by the way, is now your house. So now you can sleep in the turret. Or sell it. Or keep it and rent it out."

"Or sleep in the turret," she said excitedly. "We can fit a queen-sized bed in there!"

"Oooh, a shared turret, I'm impressed. I wasn't sure Edward was turret-worthy."

"Shut up. Stop calling me. I hate you."

"You called *me*, cousin."

"Oh, yeah. Right. Well, thanks for the turret and the house around it."

"Thanks for befriending powerful allies and killing a threat to our Pack." His voice deepened as all traces of teasing fled. "Rachael, truly. A house is a poor thank-you for what you've done for the Pack, and for me. But it's yours, and the title is in your name, so as I said, if you and Edward want to return to the Cape, you can sell it or not as you like."

"I'm not sure the Cape is ready for our return, Michael, but I'll keep all that in mind."

"I am so grateful for all that you did, and so sorry for all that you suffered. Two weeks ago I already owed you more than I could have ever repaid."

"We're family, dumbass."

"Exactly so. You already meant the world to me, and now look! Unbelievable! I am rich, Rachael, in all things. And I have you to thank for an awful lot of that. Who besides me has an accountant who can analyze a P and L statement as easily as she shatters cervical vertebrae?"

"Gross, Michael."

"I'll want to meet your mate," he added thoughtfully.

"Happened right in front of him and he *didn't* have a nervous breakdown. I won't deny being impressed."

"He did have one. He just waited until I was done with mine."

"Truly, a match made by the gods."

"I hate you."

"Just sayin'." Ah! That was better. Now he sounded more like her cousin and less like her Pack leader. "So what's up next for you?"

"Gotta go tell my man he's sleeping in a turret for a while."

"If he's anything like you've described, he's probably got his *Star Trek* posters all over it."

"*Star WARS*, Michael, get a clue."

"Sorry."

"Well, I hope so!" she cried. "That's a pretty big thing to fuck up."

"Very, very sorry."

"Okay, then."

"Okay."

"And Michael?"

"Yeah, cuz?"

"It's possible we've been sleeping in the turret because I sent the son on a month-long all-expenses-paid cruise vacation with his fiancée."

The Pack leader roared laughter and dropped his cell phone. By the time he picked it up, she was long gone, and in more ways than one.